AXES
AND
WINGS

A DARK HORIZON

LINDSAY McCAFFERTY

AXES
AND
WINGS
A DARK HORIZON

Axes and Wings: A Dark Horizon

© 2025 Lindsay McCafferty

All rights reserved.

The story, names, characters, and incidents portrayed in this production are from the author's imagination and are fictitious. No identification with actual persons (living or deceased), places, and events is intended or should be inferred.

First Edition (2025)

Cover, Logo & Title Pages designed by MiblArt

Interior format made using Atticus

ISBN-13 (Paperback): 979-8-9854011-7-2

authorlindsaymccafferty.com

PREFACE

"I want to write a book with dragons for fun." That was the thought that started this in 2023, the Year of the Dragon. After watching *House of the Dragon* and rewatching *The Hobbit* movies, I searched for any books with dwarf dragon riders. I was thinking about how dwarves like gold and dragons like gold. What if there was a story that combined *The Hobbit* and *House of the Dragon*? My search didn't yield anything, so I imagined the kind of story I wanted. This book is the manifestation of those musings.

Thank you to MiblArt for creating another marvelous cover and the title pages.

ONE

FIRELIGHT GLEAMED IN THE dark valley. Kade leaned forward in the saddle and looked around one side of Emerald's green neck. A homing pigeon had flown in after midnight with a message that Hoeckan, a dwarf settlement on the southern outskirts of Drangrere, was under attack from trolls, and the soldiers were too few and overwhelmed.

Kade had been woken from a deep sleep, armored up, and saddled Emerald. The dragon riders of Drangrere were always on call, day or night.

The chilly night air banished any sleepiness left in his body, and he had to bring his elbows in and hunch behind the saddle pommel to stay warm. Fur-lined and woolen clothes only helped so much when the wind was driven against his body through the spaces of his armor. Even the thick blue scarf wrapped around his head couldn't stop the cold from biting at his face. Emerald didn't mind the icy wind. At least the flight wouldn't be long.

He adjusted his leather goggles with glass lenses and looked to Alden, the captain, and his black dragon, Onyx. The other four riders on the team were on either side of Kade and Emerald. He pulled on one of the harness buckles, where it made his steel tasset dig into his thigh. Straps went around his waist and each leg and clipped to the saddle on either side.

As they approached the settlement, the bitter smell of smoke irritated his nose through the scarf, and he took shallower breaths. Kade spotted five trolls. Soldiers attempted to fight them off and stay clear of destroyed and burning buildings. The wooden wall had been breached at the gate and in one other place. Despite being built twice as thick, it wasn't a match for the trolls.

The creatures wore shirts, vests, and loincloths fashioned from fur pelts. Trolls had gray skin and were massive, although not as big as an adult dragon. They had sparse hair on their heads and green patches on their skin that could be mistaken for moss. A sixth troll lay dead in a heap on a smashed building, pierced by several spears.

They could only be killed by weapons like heavy spears, halberds, poleaxes, or a well-aimed bolt from a ballista, which Hoeckan was still in the process of setting up, five on the walls and one in the center. And trolls were vulnerable to dragons.

Adrenaline rushed through Kade, and his heart rate increased as the team neared the moment they would go into battle. It wasn't fear. He didn't know why he would be afraid when on the back of a large fire-breathing dragon with long, sharp talons and teeth. But this job was hazardous. What he felt was anticipation to get this done without any harm being inflicted on the team.

Alden sat up in his saddle. The riders wore silver gloves so they could give signals to each other in the dark. He gestured to Shona and Jaheem and to Kenji and Barret to fly ahead, and then he turned around and held his palm up to Kade. That meant to stay on overwatch. Kade nodded and pulled his spear out from its holder on his back.

"Stay above, Em," Kade called to his dragon.

He kept his left hand wrapped around the bar on the pommel of the saddle and gripped the spear with his right. The cold air was now the furthest thing from his mind. Emerald circled above the settlement as the other dragons began their descent to attack. They positioned themselves to be upwind of the smoke.

An enormous troll raised its stone club to crush the soldiers in front of it, but then Onyx swooped in, scooped the brute up with the talons on her back legs, and closed her jaws around its neck. Blood showered the ground as she ripped into the troll and dropped the body. Only she could pull off that move because of her large size. Being one hundred and ninety years old with tons of fighting experience helped, too.

Jaheem's red dragon, Ruby, stooped onto a troll with a stolen dwarf halberd and knocked it to the ground. The weapon went flying end over end down the street, and soldiers dived out of the way to avoid getting hit. As Ruby delivered the killing bite, another troll roared and ran at her, its stone spear raised. Jade, Kenji's dark green dragon, struck it from the side.

The other two trolls gripped their clubs and watched the skies, their attention off the soldiers and residents and on the circling dragons overhead. The dwarves on the ground backed off, giving the dragon riders room to work.

Topaz, Shona's light blue dragon, stooped at a troll, but it had figured out the game. This was far from the team's first battle, though. As Topaz swooped close by, the troll stepped to the side and swiped at him with its club, but the agile dragon twisted out of the way at the last moment.

A juke. Smoky, Barret's swift gray dragon, attacked the distracted troll a couple of seconds behind Topaz. But he didn't pin the brute all the way down, and it raised its club. Barret threw his spear, and the weapon sank into the troll's chest, making it drop the club. Then Smoky went in for the kill.

The light blue dragon quickly pivoted and stooped at the last troll, but it was in a tight space. Shona yelled for Topaz to fire, and the brute screamed as flames enveloped it. It stumbled back a few steps and fell on a burning building.

Kade smiled. The trolls were dead. The team was unscathed. Dwarves below cheered. Then Kade saw a shape lurking on the edge of the tree line south of Hoeckan. Emerald turned her head toward it, too. Something large and gray hid in the shadows. Another troll.

"Go get it, Emerald."

She stooped toward the troll, and it ran into the woods. Emerald glided over the trees, searching for a large enough clearing to get the drop on it. Kade spotted one up ahead. "There, girl. Get in front of the troll."

Emerald folded her wings and raced to the clearing. His dragon was only sixty, but she was skilled in battle. As she turned around, the troll appeared at the tree line but not far enough out for Emerald to attack.

Kade aimed and threw his spear at the same time that his dragon pulled up to avoid the trees. The troll cried out as the weapon slammed into its left shoulder. The injury would be devastating because the heavy spearhead had the force and momentum of a dragon behind it.

Emerald turned and dived back toward the clearing, but the troll ran into the trees again and headed toward the Dragon's Tail Mountain Range and wild lands. Kade spotted Ruby and Topaz flying toward him. They joined him in the chase, but the troll was nowhere to be found. It might have hunkered down in the woods or hidden in a cave. The three eventually turned their dragons toward the settlement.

Hoeckan was fairly new, built for its proximity to a coal mine. Because most of the structures were wooden, the trolls had destroyed half of the buildings and homes, and several bodies lay scattered. Without the dragons, it could've been worse.

The riders had done their duty, and Kade was proud of his team. But then the cold crept back in.

They were only managing an increasing recurring problem and not fixing it.

TWO

PRINCESS GRIFFIN STOOD IN the skywalk, watching for the dragon riders' return. The long hallway stuck out from a mountain and had open windows on one side. Griffin could see her breath in the chilly February morning air, but she was warm in her blue long-sleeved dress, blue fur-lined cloak, and black pants.

She rubbed the silver dragon pendant on her necklace with her fingers as yearning filled her heart whenever she thought of those creatures. Drangrere's standard featured a dragon, but the members of the royal family weren't allowed to be riders. It was too dangerous. But a girl could dream, and for twenty-seven years, Griffin had.

To fly through the air and view the world from the back of a dragon must be breathtaking. She would love to see the stronghold from above, as well as the Blood Spear Mountains. The views from the two tall watchtowers didn't suffice.

And the fights would be exciting. The dragon riders primarily defended settlements from trolls or goblins, and sometimes, they aided travelers and caravans. But the last two could only be helped if the riders noticed trouble while out on patrol, or someone got to a settlement and sent a message to the stronghold. They also chased off any wild dragons that strayed into Drangrere. Although, that was rare.

Her royal status couldn't stop her from enjoying the company of the dragons. Griffin spotted five shapes in the sky. She grinned. They were all back and heading to the eyrie. Griffin picked her skirt up and hurried down the skywalk to meet them, her guard trailing after her. The dragon wings protruding from the sides of the helmets that the royal guards wore distinguished them from the soldiers.

Griffin stopped at the door. "Wait in the hall," she told the guard. He was new.

"Yes, Princess."

She entered the large, cavernous room as the dragons entered one by one through the big doors and went to their nests. The tightness in her chest left after she saw that all the riders were unharmed.

Crystal, a white dragon with pale blue eyes, barely lifted her head to acknowledge the others, even when Topaz nuzzled her. Poor thing. She missed Ada. Crystal was curled up in her nest, which was a dip carved into the granite floor and filled with hay and large brown and black terror bird feathers.

The mountains had been filled with red granite with golden-and-black flecks, so most of the stronghold was carved from it. Although in the eyrie, the polished floors were full of patterns of scratches from the dragons' talons. The massive space was lit by skylights and windows. It had, to a certain extent, been a natural cave that was expanded. Stalactites hung from the ceiling, and stalagmites jutted up here and there next to the walls.

Griffin went to Kade as he dismounted. The riders wore long-sleeved chain mail shirts and lighter armor than the soldiers. Each pant leg was one of the kingdom's colors, blue and silver.

Kade undid the chinstrap of his helmet and removed his headgear. He had brown eyes, straight black hair that went past his ears, and a short beard. He always said that shorter hair was easier to deal with as a dragon rider. Otherwise, he would have to tie it back or braid it, like a few of the others did.

Kade noticed she was there and bowed his head. "Hey, Griffin."

"Did you all take care of the trolls?"

"Yeah." Then he frowned. "One got away with my spear in its shoulder."

"Oh, well, you have extras. That's not a big loss."

Kade shrugged. "I still would've preferred not to have lost it."

Wheels creaked as Jaheem and Barret closed the big doors. There were two on each side to make the process easier. Emerald made a rumbling noise like a purr and stared at Griffin with big green eyes. While Kade took off the saddlebags, the weapons, and the saddle, she petted the dragon on her head.

"Good girl. You're such a sweetie pie." Warm breath from Emerald's nostrils blew over her.

A lot of dwarves feared the dragons and saw them as ferocious beasts, but Griffin loved everything about them. Their magnificent presence, their intelligence, their amazing ability to breathe fire, and the horns on their heads and rows of spikes on their necks and tails that made them look so fierce.

Emerald had the body of a regular adult female dragon, as well as her sister, Ruby. Crystal and Smoky, who were mother and son, had more angular physiques, although the white dragon was small for an adult female. Jade was bulkier, and Topaz's spikes and horns were longer.

Kade set the saddle on its rack and opened his mouth to say something, but then several royal guards walked into the eyrie, along with Griffin's father, King Magus. Kade bowed.

Her dad was fifty-five and had ruled for twenty years. He had brown eyes, brown wavy hair that was graying and went past his shoulders, and a long beard that went to his chest. The other riders stopped what they were doing.

Alden went to greet him. The captain of the dragon riders was forty and had brown eyes, long, straight, dark brown hair that was partly braided back, and a short beard. He bowed his head. "My king."

"I thought you all would have been home earlier." Her dad glanced nervously at the dragons and kept away from the nests. He didn't come to the eyrie often.

"We stayed for a while to help with the cleanup. The trolls breached the gate and broke through one part of the wall. Hoeckan's ballistae weren't set up yet."

Her dad nodded and seemed unfazed. "It sounds like we're on the right track with the new defenses if, besides the gate, the wall was only broken in one place. Were the trolls dispatched?"

Alden's eyes filled with frustration. "One escaped, but the others were killed."

Griffin's dad grinned and clapped his hands together. "Very good. You and your team make Drangrere proud of your brave service. How severe was the damage to Hoeckan?"

Alden frowned. He wore that expression constantly lately. The wrinkles on his face seemed to be deeper and the shadows under his eyes darker. Griffin wondered if he had slept sufficiently lately.

"The trolls destroyed half of the buildings and killed over a dozen civilians and soldiers," Alden said.

"But the coal mine is fine, right?"

The captain furrowed his brow even more. "Yes. But it will take weeks to rebuild and fortify the settlement. We also need to talk about building an eyrie on the other side of the kingdom to help with patrols and protection of the settlements farther away."

Her dad shook his head.

"My lord, please. We have three hatchlings and two eggs. When settlements nearer to the eastern border are in trouble, my team can't always reach them fast enough to prevent significant damage and loss of life. And because we're building new ones faster than normal in wilder areas, the attacks have been at a higher rate."

"Daddy," Griffin said, "maybe we should build another eyrie for the good of the kingdom. Jorungir and Vuustwern have two."

"No," he said firmly and put a hand on Alden's shoulder, but his face was stony. "We are at more peace than we've ever been now that we have an alliance with King Bogden's faction of goblins in Gristnak. The new wall design is proving its worth, and with enough ballistae, settlements should be nigh impenetrable. The trolls will learn to stay away. In the meantime, we can focus more on mining riches and resources and expanding the kingdom. Building another eyrie is unnecessary and costly." He patted Alden's shoulder.

"The farther we expand into the wilderness, far from the stronghold, the harder our ability to protect the settlements will be. And this new process of building almost everything from wood first. Respectfully, my lord, I don't think it's a good idea. Even when extra ballistae are set up, the trolls know how to avoid them."

Her dad pressed his lips together, and his eyes grew darker. "Do you seek to make me and this kingdom look weak, Captain Alden?"

"Of course not, your grace."

"Are you saying that your team is ineffective at their job?"

Alden raised his eyebrows. "No, your grace, I'm just—"

"Then there's nothing to worry about. Keep up the great work," her dad said tensely and left with his guards.

Alden sighed. He looked even more weary. "You all can rest. The saddles can be cleaned later. Nice spear throw, Barret."

"Thank you, sir." The rider's blue eyes lit up, and he looked proud of himself. Barret had ginger wavy hair that went past his shoulders and was in one large braid, with two smaller ones next to it. He had a short beard with a braid under his chin.

"Kade, grab a new spear before we go on another call for help," Alden said as he walked by.

"Yes, sir."

"Princess." Alden bowed his head to her.

"Make sure you rest, too, Captain," Griffin said.

Alden nodded, but his thoughts seemed to be elsewhere. He walked with a slumped posture.

Griffin went up to Kade. "Was it really that bad at Hoeckan?" she asked.

He grimaced. "They're not that far, but the defenses weren't fully constructed. That did them no favors." He put his weapons on the rack on the wall. The single-headed axe and the knife would go to his quarters with him. The rest of the team left the eyrie, and the dragons lay in their nests to nap.

Perfect. They were alone. "Is Alden right?"

Kade opened and closed his mouth and seemed hesitant.

"We've been friends for years. I know I'm the princess, but it's just us. You can tell me."

Kade nodded. "Yes. Your father may believe that building with wood first is faster and can be as protective as stone if it's thick enough, but it doesn't always work. It can still be smashed through, which probably emboldens trolls to attack more often, and then once the brutes are drawn in, they have more conflicts with older settlements. And more ballistae make no difference unless a troll is caught by surprise. It would be nice if we could go back to building with stone first and not hurrying to move dwarves in. The mild winter this year isn't helping either. Another eyrie would help us with patrols and dealing with attacks. And I worry about Hoeckan. There's a pass in the Dragon's Tail Mountains that opens into Raggerath. King Nafrag's goblins could stroll right in, and Hoeckan would be a sitting duck. Can you talk with your father about it? You may have more luck convincing him."

"I'll try. But he's dead set that his plan will work. And he won't admit that he's wrong." Griffin wanted to believe her dad that everything was fine with the settlements, but she knew to listen to Kade. They had known each other since they were children, after his father had been reassigned to the stronghold. Kade was like a brother to her. At twenty-five years old, he could've been a good suitor for her were he not a dragon rider.

Speaking of relationships. "Have you introduced yourself to Maysie yet?"

Kade blushed and looked away. "No."

"Why not? She's pretty, and Jane said that she's nice."

Kade stroked Emerald's neck. "I don't know what to say to her."

"You can start with, 'Hello, my name is Kade, and I'm a badass dragon rider.'"

"How is that so easy for you?"

Griffin smiled. "Because I know how to be bold and speak up for myself. That's how I get what I want."

"You always get what you want."

Except for riding a dragon. She was still working on that one. Griffin patted Emerald one more time and frowned. "I'm not sure about the second eyrie and changing how the settlements are built." She pointed at him. "Go and meet Maysie the first chance you get. Don't make me force you."

Kade bowed his head. "Yes, ma'am."

Griffin left and tried to work out in her head how to convince her stubborn dad to provide what the dragon riders said the kingdom needed.

THREE

LATER THAT NIGHT, KADE had the duty of feeding the hatchlings, and then he was done for the day, unless he was going to be yanked out of bed again to go on a call. He hoped tonight would be quiet. Kade made sure the candle sconces on the walls were lit. The riders needed the light if they had to come into the eyrie at night.

As he approached the eyrie door, he spotted his team members crowded in front of the meeting room that the riders called their war room. Kade closed the door and went to see what was going on.

"Hey," he said, "what are you guys doing?"

Jaheem turned to him. "He's at it again." The rider was a year older than Kade and had brown eyes, long black locs that were tied back, and a short beard.

Kade squeezed past Barret and Shona to look through the door that was cracked open. The war room was filled with maps, books, and records of the lineage of the dragons. Hanging on one wall were scales in shadowboxes from dragons who had died. The room was lit by candlelight and a small fireplace. A skylight would let sunlight in during the day. Alden sat at a large round table in the middle of the room. He seemed so consumed by what he was doing that he didn't realize his team was watching him.

A map of the kingdom was spread out on the table that had locations marked with red X's where there had been attacks in the past few months. Alden stared at the map and muttered to himself too softly for Kade to hear. This had started after Ada was killed.

"Let's leave him alone," Barret said. "There's nothing we can do when he's like this." He quietly closed the door.

"It's because he cares so much," Kade said.

Shona frowned. She had brown eyes and long, wavy black hair that was braided back. She was twenty-seven. "With the attack rate increasing, it seems hopeless that we can effectively defend the settlements. It wasn't this bad when I joined the team seven years ago."

Jaheem shook his head. "You have to think more positively, Shona."

"I'm being realistic."

"Kenji, how about you? Any thoughts about what we can do?"

The twenty-nine-year-old dwarf with hazel eyes, short, straight black hair, and a short beard pursed his lips and shook his head. He spoke little.

Barret crossed his arms. "The king has to do something. We can't keep going on like this." He sighed. "Come on, let's go to bed."

"What gives you the right to tell us what to do?" Jaheem protested.

Barret lifted his chin. "Because I'm the oldest."

The door to the war room abruptly opened, and Alden paused mid-stride with a dazed look. Then he furrowed his brow. "You all should rest in case we have to fly out to battle tonight. Again."

"Yes, sir," Barret said. "We're going now." He herded them toward their quarters, which were down a hallway leading off of the skywalk.

They needed to stay near the eyrie. Each set of quarters was for a single person. There were larger ones for if a rider was married with children, but they were empty at the moment.

"I can't stay, boys," Shona said. "I've got a date to get to." She went into her quarters to probably change.

Kade hoped tonight would be quiet, and the team would get some well-deserved rest.

FOUR

WITHIN THE NEXT FEW days, Barret, Shona, Kade, and Alden had to rush to East Pass, on the other side of the kingdom, where there was a goblin attack on a caravan of dwarves near the eastern border. They had been transporting iron, coal, and one large wagon filled with copper and silver.

Jaheem and Kenji were gone on patrol. The attack had been over by the time the riders arrived. There had been minimal casualties, but most of the cargo had been stolen.

The goblins weren't from Raggerath, as far as anyone could tell. It wasn't unusual for roving groups to carry out attacks. In contrast to the trolls' primal need to survive, goblins preyed mostly on travelers to steal cargo for their own gain, which was why the riders were sometimes asked to escort caravans depending on the route and items being transported. Alden had spent the rest of the day in the war room, obsessing over his map and trying to unravel a messy pattern.

The next day, Kade was sweeping hay and feathers that Ruby, Emerald, and Onyx had scattered outside of their nests, as well as in the middle of the room. Kenji had cleaned the other side and then went to get the new spear from the blacksmiths for Kade.

There had been no spares left. The other rider had also wanted to visit with his brother, Riku. Barret and Shona were on patrol. Alden was most likely in the war room, and Kade wasn't sure where Jaheem was.

The eyrie was quiet except for Jade's snores. A chilly breeze blew in from the open big doors. He stepped on a large feather before it tumbled away and tossed it back into Emerald's nest. Kade wore thick leather gloves and a blue fur-lined leather coat over his blue-and-silver tunic.

He heard heavy steps and talons scraping and clicking on the floor behind him. Ruby had come in from a smaller, curved passageway that led to the mountainside. Her jaws were wet, so she had gotten a drink of water. The dragons could come and go as they pleased.

They generally stayed close to the eyrie, though. The dragons learned from birth that this was their home. While Kade watched Ruby pass by and go to her nest next to Emerald, the broom was snatched from his hand.

"Hey."

Emerald held the broom in her mouth like a dog holding a prized stick.

"Emerald, give it back," Kade said firmly.

The dragon lowered her head and then snapped it back up before he could grab the broom. Kade crossed his arms, and Emerald made a sound as if she was laughing. Ruby watched with amusement in her red eyes.

"Oh, yeah. Very funny. You know what? I don't want it." Kade turned his back on his dragon and tried to hide his amusement. "Nope. Who cares about a silly broom?"

Wait for it. As expected, the broom clattered on the floor, and a nose bumped him in the back. Kade turned around with a smile and stroked Emerald's snout. She looked at him with a soft expression and adoring eyes.

It was said that dragon eyes were cold, but that was by people who spent little time with them. They weren't devoid of emotions, like Crystal's vacant eyes and slack expression.

Kade walked over to the depressed white dragon, who lay in her nest. She glanced at him for a moment and then looked away. Kade sat next to her head and petted her. The white dragon was one of the sweetest-tempered ones he knew.

"Hey, Crystal. I know you miss Ada. The rest of us do, too."

The dragon groaned.

"You can have all the time you want to grieve before we find you a new rider."

Crystal sighed. Griffin entered the eyrie and came over to them. She wore a green dress and a green fur-lined cloak, which she drew tighter around herself when the breeze hit her. Her blond, wavy hair was braided back, and concern filled her blue eyes.

"Is she okay?"

"Yeah. Or I don't know. She eats and goes outside now and again, but she can't tell us how she feels."

Griffin sat on the other side of Crystal's head and rubbed her. "How many months has it been?"

"Six." Kade shook his head and grimaced. "That day was terrible for us. I don't blame Crystal for feeling like this. It was Alden and Ada's last day escorting a caravan that was transporting gold and gemstones north to the Jorungir border, and then that group of goblins had to attack. In her ninety years, Crystal has had three riders, but Ada was the only one she had to witness bleed out and die on her back from an arrow to the throat. It took us hours to wash the blood from her scales. And Alden was inconsolable. I'm sure he was going to propose to Ada. One day, I spotted him looking at rings with a jeweler." Griffin rubbed her gold engagement ring. Kade felt a pang of sadness. "I keep forgetting that you're moving to Carodhall in a few months."

She got a wistful look in her eyes. "I can't get over feeling sad and excited about it. There'll be new places to see and new friends to make, but I'll miss you and the dragons. The wedding at Carodhall may be the last time we'll spend a lot of time with each other."

His stomach felt hollow, and he looked away for a moment as he rubbed Crystal's neck. Griffin had been such a good friend, his first friend in the stronghold. "You know, they have a team of dragons at Carodhall. The orange one, Tourmaline, is Onyx's baby. We traded him for Crystal when we had too many males. He's quite large, although his mama is big for a female."

"And do you think the captain will allow me to hang out with them like Alden does?"

Kade shrugged. "You've always gotten along with them. I'll put in a good word for you."

"Thanks." She stared at her engagement ring again, but her expression looked a little sad.

"You do love him, right?" Kade asked.

Griffin gave him a glowing smile. "I've always wanted to marry a prince, and Erik is everything I could have hoped for. I'll be happy to spend the rest of my life with him, but I still desire to be a dragon rider." She patted Crystal on the head. "Had I not been noble born, I would've had a chance to be one. That dream won't ever leave me. But as I'm constantly reminded, my place is as a royal and eventual queen of Carodhall."

"Did you have any luck with your father, by the way?"

Griffin frowned and shook her head. "I used every trick I know, and I couldn't convince him. He won't budge on his opinion that the kingdom is the safest and most powerful it's ever been, and it's time to expand and increase our wealth." She huffed. "If I didn't talk with you and the team to find out what's going on out there, I would never realize how bad things are."

Crystal lifted her head and stood. Kade and Griffin stepped out of the way as she headed toward the side door.

"She's probably going to sun herself." Kade crossed his arms as a shiver went through him. He wouldn't mind joining her. Griffin stared longingly at Crystal.

"Hey, do you want to visit the hatchlings?" Kade asked. "It'll be warmer in the nursery."

That seemed to cheer her up because she nodded excitedly with a grin.

FIVE

THE NURSERY WAS AT the back of the eyrie. Griffin followed Kade through the door and into the smaller room. He was distracting her, and she appreciated it.

The nursery had a lower ceiling and a few stalactites and stalagmites, most of which were broken. There were stone platforms on the walls. A few on the ground had multiple pieces attached to a central pole, like a tree. They had to be stone because, considering the amount of scorch marks on the walls and the floor where the hatchlings had been overexuberant while playing, wood would be a bad idea. Even the chest in the corner was stone. The door had steel plates on the inside.

There were three large windows on the left side of the room. Two of the hatchlings sat on a sill and stared outside. They turned their heads, squealed excitedly, and flew toward Kade and Griffin. The largest was Cobalt, who was black with amber eyes. His brother Sandstone was tan with light brown eyes. They were Onyx's babies.

Cobalt resembled her in looks. The father was thought to be a wild dragon because Onyx's mate, Agate, had died years ago. Dragons usually mated for life, but sometimes, they just wanted to breed. Onyx and Agate had had Topaz, Jade, and Tourmaline.

The youngest hatchling, Sapphire, was in the nest at the back of the nursery. She also hurried toward them. Her mother was Ruby, and her father was a dragon from the Nalmere team called Turquoise. Jaheem had stayed there for a couple of days when he delivered a message to the king. According to him, Turquoise and Ruby had been very affectionate with each other.

"Hello, little ones." Griffin picked up Sapphire, who had landed at her feet. Her scales and eyes were blue. The hatchlings were still small enough to hold. All of them weren't even a year old and wouldn't be able to bear a rider until they were five or six.

"Watch the talons and the spikes," Kade warned. He held Sandstone in his arms, and Cobalt sat on his shoulder. The black hatchling regarded everything with a deeply thoughtful look, seeming as serious as his mother.

"I have a cat. I know all about claws." Griffin flipped Sapphire over so her arm was around the hatchling's back, where nothing was sharp. "Is she named after one of the first dragons we had?"

"Yes. This Sapphire is descended from her namesake through Ruby. Flynn and Lucas took an enormous risk when they found those eggs and decided to raise dragons in captivity."

"Why?"

"Well, when Sapphire and Moonstone hatched, how would the brothers have known if the hatchlings would perceive them as friends or food?"

Griffin giggled as Cobalt jumped onto her shoulder and rubbed his head against hers. "Clearly, when raised by us, they see us as friends."

Griffin stroked Sapphire on her belly. Her scales were soft, which was one reason the hatchlings were always supervised when they were let outside until they grew larger. Sapphire purred with delight. She reached up with a little wing foot, trying to grab the dragon pendant.

"Careful. She'll take it," Kade said.

Sapphire pulled on the pendant.

"No. Let's not play with that, sweetie." Griffin got it away and slid it under her dress, out of sight. The hatchling squeaked in protest. "The other dragons ignore it at this point. I keep forgetting that I need to hide anything that I don't want the babies to mess with."

Dragons had a fascination with shiny rocks, gems, and metals. These had to be covered while being transported. Wild dragons had stolen whole cart or wagon loads of anything shiny, even coins. That's why the riders wore little jewelry around their mounts.

Sapphire squirmed, and Griffin set her down. Cobalt jumped off her shoulder, and the two hatchlings wrestled on the floor. Sandstone watched lazily from Kade's arms. Griffin walked over to a trough with raised edges that was filled with hay and feathers.

An orange egg and a white egg sat in the cradle. They looked like large gemstones. Crystal had birthed them a few days before Ada's death. Her mate was Topaz.

Griffin touched the eggs. They were naturally warm and only required a safe place to incubate until hatching time, which took six to seven months. "Will the eggs hatch soon?"

Kade put Sandstone down, and the hatchling fluttered over to his nursery mates. "They should." He joined Griffin and felt each egg. "The scary thing is checking if they're warm. If they go cold, the baby has died. It happens often. Twenty years ago, Crystal gave birth to three eggs, but Smoky was the only one who hatched. The others died within the first couple of months. These two have made it this long, so they should be okay."

Griffin touched each egg. The heat stung her skin a little but didn't burn her. "Have you all picked names yet?"

"For the orange one, either Sunstone or Amber. And for the white one, either Quartz or Diamond."

"Let me know when they're going to hatch."

"As long as we notice in time."

She hoped the eggs hatched before she left. There was a scrabbling sound. Cobalt was in a large trough full of wood shavings, getting ready to do his business. Griffin let out a sly smile when Kade wasn't looking. Time for the real reason she had sought out her friend. "Kade, come with me. There's something I want to show you."

SIX

KADE FOLLOWED GRIFFIN OUT of the eyrie and into the stronghold. Her guard kept a respectful distance back. As a rider, he rarely had a reason to leave the confines of the eyrie, despite his team's insistence that he needed to get out more. Why did he need to when he was perfectly content being around the dragons?

Like most dwarf kingdoms, Drangrere was a city built inside the mountains. They walked through passages, hallways, and up and down stairs, working their way through crowds of dwarves. When he had first arrived here with his parents, it was like a maze. In the center of the stronghold was the great hall.

They walked by a stream that gurgled from one opening in the wall to another. Dwarves were masters of stone, but between all the patterns carved onto the walls and doorways, mostly of dragons and soldiers, the builders left natural features, like the glittering gypsum flowers he had passed.

He heard clanging and plinking from miners and artisans here and there. Firelight, natural shafts of sunlight, and strategically placed windows and skylights lit most of the stronghold. Kade preferred the open skies, even if that was considered by some to be unusual for a dwarf.

Griffin led him to the tall windows that looked out over the stronghold gate and courtyard. "Maysie," she called.

Kade halted. Maysie, the girl he'd been putting off meeting. She turned around from where she was staring out a window and bowed to Griffin. Maysie had curly red hair and blue eyes. She wore a light blue dress with a pink sash tied around her waist, black boots, bracelets on both wrists, earrings, and a necklace.

"Kade," Griffin said as they walked up to her, "this is Maysie."

"Hello, Kade," Maysie said. She held out her hand.

His mind froze, and it took a moment longer than necessary to process what he was supposed to do. He shook her hand and swallowed nervously. She was beautiful, but he didn't know her. Another awkward moment passed.

"Say something," Griffin muttered.

"Hello." In his mind, he face-palmed himself.

Maysie smiled at him, and he returned it as best he could while attempting to keep his nerves under control. Why did he feel so hot?

"Well, I'll leave you two to get acquainted," Griffin said. "I have business to attend to."

Kade watched wide-eyed as Griffin left. She threw a smug smile at him before she disappeared into the crowd. He turned back to Maysie.

"So, uh, what do you do?" Was that a stupid question to start with? He should have asked one of his team members or Shona's boyfriend, Roger, for advice a long time ago.

"I work with my mother, Odette. She's a jeweler, and my father, Quinn, is a miner. I've lived in the stronghold my whole life."

Kade nodded. "I guess you know that I'm a dragon rider. I came here with my parents when I was young. They moved back to Gereten to help with family members. My father's a soldier." He shoved his hands in his pockets when he felt them trembling.

"Do you like being a dragon rider?"

"Yes, I love it." Finally, a subject he could speak confidently about. "I've dreamed of being a rider since I was a child. I know dragons may seem scary, but they're loving and loyal, and they're really cool to work with. You could meet my dragon, Emerald, if you want to."

She gave a small smile. "That would be interesting."

They stood in silence again. Maysie looked out a window, and Kade did too, as he tried to come up with something to say. He knew little about jewelry or mining.

"So, my mom's going to be expecting me to come back to the shop soon," Maysie said abruptly. "We could meet up again at some point."

"Yes. I don't always know when I have to leave, but I'm sure we can figure out something."

"Whenever you have a chance, come find me."

Kade nodded, his stomach fluttering. "Okay. That sounds great."

"It was nice to meet you." She grinned.

"Nice to meet you, too." Kade sighed as she walked away. It was a miracle that she wanted to see him again.

"Was she cute?" Jaheem asked as he and Kade walked toward their quarters later that evening.

Kade blushed. "Yeah."

The other rider wrapped an arm around his shoulders. "Did you make plans to meet her again?"

"She told me to come see her the next chance I get."

"Your first girlfriend," Jaheem grinned and patted his shoulder.

"Who has a girlfriend?" Shona asked as she passed them.

"Kade," Jaheem said proudly.

Shona smiled. "Congratulations, Kade. If you need any advice from a woman's perspective, let me know."

"Thanks," he said, embarrassed about his team members fussing over him. Shona went into her quarters.

"Our little boy is finally growing up," Jaheem said. "I wasn't sure when this would happen. I mean, you're kind, handsome, although not as handsome as me, and you're a dragon rider, but I was starting to think that I'd have to set you up with a date."

"I'm so nervous around her. I'm nervous around every new person, but her even more."

Jaheem went to stand in front of him as they reached his quarters. "You need to show confidence. Girls like that. You're not scared of the dragons. Imagine her as Emerald. Actually, no." He waved his hands. "Bad metaphor."

"I get it. Talk with her like I talk with dwarves I know well."

Jaheem patted him on the chest. "Make me proud."

Wooing a girl felt more difficult than flying a dragon into battle.

SEVEN

"NO. FOR THE HUNDREDTH time, the answer is no, Griffin."

"But, Mom, please."

Griffin was with her mom in the quarters shared by the members of the royal family. All the rooms were connected and luxuriously furnished. Griffin and her mom stood in the living room. Queen Helga was fifty-three, had long, straight blond hair that was graying and blue eyes that were filled with annoyance. They wore their night gowns and had been about to go to bed, but then Griffin brought up the seemingly impossible question. Could she ride a dragon?

"But, Mom, I won't be in Drangrere much longer. This is my last chance. One ride. That's all I'm asking. Then I'll never bring it up again," Griffin implored with her best pleading expression.

Her mom crossed her arms. "Do you know what happened to Prince Riker of Jorungir after he decided he wanted to become a dragon rider?"

Griffin knew the story, but her mom was going to recount it anyway.

"Barely a week in, a terror bird plucked him off his dragon's back. The safety straps didn't stop him from being pulled out of the saddle and dropped to his death."

It wasn't just about tradition that royals didn't become riders. Her mom feared something terrible would happen to her child. Griffin couldn't fault her for that. She softened her tone. "He was alone. I would ride with Kade. He'll keep me safe. Think of it as a wedding gift."

Her mom looked away and ran a hand across the side of her face but seemed to consider it. Griffin crossed her fingers behind her back. She hadn't gotten this far before with her previous requests, but that never discouraged her from continuing to try. Inheriting her dad's stubbornness served her well.

"All right," her mom said.

Griffin held back a squeal, and her body seemed to vibrate with joy. Yes! All the years of asking, praying to the gods, and being patient had paid off. She was so happy that she could jump around and shout with glee. She could run through the hallways and tell anyone who would listen that she, Princess Griffin of Drangrere, was going to ride a dragon. Then her mom would fuss that that behavior wasn't proper, and she wouldn't care.

"But it has to be with Kade or one of the other riders. Not by yourself," her mom said sternly.

"Of course." Griffin hugged her. "Thank you, Mom."

"I still have to talk with your father. I can't guarantee that he'll say yes."

Griffin pulled away. "But he couldn't disappoint me after you gave your permission."

She heard a trill behind her, and a fluffy gray tabby cat with yellow eyes sauntered toward her, rubbing on the leg of a chair on his way. Sir Whiskers, her bestest friend in the entire world. She had found him five years ago when he was a kitten. He had been huddling next to the stone rampart of the stronghold on a snowy winter afternoon. How he'd ended up there was unknown.

Sir Whiskers meowed and rubbed against Griffin's legs. She picked him up. "I would take you flying with me, but I don't think you'd like it."

Her mom reached one hand out to pet him, but he swatted at her. She pressed her lips together. "I won't miss this cantankerous beast."

"At least he doesn't growl or hiss at you."

Her mom kissed her on the head, keeping well away from Sir Whiskers. "Good night, my dear."

"Good night. And I really appreciate you letting me ride a dragon."

Her mom nodded, but worry shone in her eyes.

Griffin ended up lying awake for a long time that night. She was too wound up with excitement. Sir Whiskers had moved to the foot of the bed, probably annoyed with her constant fidgeting. She couldn't believe that all her dreams would come true.

EIGHT

T HE NEXT DAY WAS quiet for the dragon riders, thank the gods. After sunset, Kade went into the eyrie to see Emerald one more time before he went to bed. The big doors were open, and Alden stood at the edge of the drop-off. Kade walked toward him, stroking Emerald's head on the way. The captain didn't seem to notice him. Onyx rumbled in greeting as Kade approached.

"Captain?"

Alden flinched and turned around. He held a cup in his hand. "I'm sorry, Kade. I didn't hear you coming. Do you need something?"

"No. I was checking if you wanted help with closing the doors." And to make certain that he was okay.

Alden looked as though his mind was elsewhere. "Thank you, Kade. I just needed some air." The captain went over and picked up a jug of mead from the floor. He refilled his cup and then held the jug out to Kade.

"No, sir. I don't want any."

Alden's gaze was pensive. "I talked with the king again. He thinks I'm being paranoid." He huffed, and his eyes flashed with anger. "The dwarf lords and ladies sit on their riches and grow fat and complacent. Protected in their strongholds, they know nothing of the dangers of the world, and they are blind to the sacrifices others make to keep them safe." Alden's voice trembled on the last few words.

Onyx whined and stared at her rider with worry in her amber eyes. Alden turned toward the drop-off again. Kade glanced over his shoulder at the door to make sure there were no unexpected listeners. The last thing they needed was for one of the team to be accused of slander against the royals.

When Alden spoke again, his voice was steadier, but he had a faraway look in his eyes, "But I guess even dragon riders can't change the ways of the world. I've analyzed the attacks on the map for months, trying to find a pattern of where trolls and goblins are more likely to attack. But they're all over the place. I don't know how to make us any more effective than we already are, and that's not disparagement directed toward you or the others. These problems are out of our control."

"I understand, sir," Kade said. "I think I can speak on the team's behalf when I say that we will fight as hard as possible to keep this kingdom safe, no matter the risks."

Alden gave him an approving nod and stared at him curiously. "You're a brave young dwarf, Kade. I'm glad to have you on this team. Have you ever thought about becoming the captain one day?"

Kade was lost for words for a moment. "No. I'm not the most senior member to replace you."

"Age has nothing to do with who should be a leader. Passion, dedication, honor. That's what it means to be a leader."

He appreciated his captain's compliment, but he could barely talk to a girl. How would he lead a team? Barret was a better choice. He had the confidence and bravado to do the job, and he was the oldest after Alden.

The captain took a long drink from his cup. "Run along to bed, Kade. I have a lot to think about. I can close the doors by myself."

"Good night, sir."

"Hmm," was all Alden said.

NINE

K ADE WALKED INTO THE eyrie the next morning and stopped in surprise. Alden wore his armor, and Onyx was saddled. He was filling the bags on either side of the cantle with supplies.

"Magus gave me permission to leave," he said after he noticed Kade. "He wasn't pleased to be woken from his bed so early, but I think he's glad I won't be pestering him for a while. I'm going to patrol the borders and speak with some of the other teams."

"How long will you be gone?"

"A couple of weeks, maybe more. I need to get a better sense of what's going on out there. You'll be acting captain in my absence."

Kade's stomach seemed to drop, and his breath caught in his throat. "Are you sure? What about Barret?"

Alden came up to him. His jaw was set, and he looked more resolute than he had been in weeks. "As sure as I'll ever be. Barret has potential, but you're frequently the first to arrive at the eyrie and the last to leave. You do menial tasks without complaint. And you've led patrols before. The others are fine soldiers, and I don't doubt them for a second. But you have care and consideration even deeper than them. We need that right now."

Kade's chest tightened. "I don't know if I can do this."

Alden put his hands on Kade's shoulders and looked him in the eyes. "I knew from the moment I interviewed you that you had the potential to be a leader, even if you don't see it. Remember what the princess keeps telling you. Be confident in yourself."

Kade wasn't sure if that made him feel better or more afraid. "I'll do my best."

Alden nodded, grabbed his headgear, and went to Onyx's right side. The nests in the floor brought the dragons lower so they were easier to mount.

"Sir, do you want to let Cobalt and Sandstone see their mother before you leave?"

"I already did." He put a foot on Onyx's wing but then hesitated. "When I became a dragon rider, the only thing I feared was failing my team," he said wistfully. "Now, I fear failing everyone in this kingdom. With any luck, I'll be back with new ideas, maybe some the king will listen to." He mounted Onyx and readied himself to leave.

The familiar chill ran through Kade when he thought about the increasing attacks. "Fly safe, Captain. We'll be waiting for your return."

"Keep the team safe. Fly, Onyx."

That's the part that scared Kade even more. It wasn't just about him watching his team members' backs. He was now responsible for their lives. Leading a patrol and running the eyrie were two very different challenges. As he watched Onyx fly off, Kade didn't hear the rest of the team come in.

"Where's Alden going?" Barret asked.

Just like the captain last night, Kade flinched. The team stared at him with curious expressions. "He's going on an extended patrol and to visit other teams. He may not be back for a couple of weeks or more."

"Okay," Jaheem said. "So, we're a man down temporarily. We can manage."

Barret walked toward Smoky. "Let's get started with our duties. Jaheem and Kade, the hatchlings need to be fed, and the floor needs to be swept. I'll lead a morning patrol with Kenji and Shona. Kade, why are you standing there looking so nervous?"

"Alden made me the acting captain."

The others stared at him in surprise and said nothing for a moment. Then Kenji walked up to him. Kade was curious about what he would say.

"I believe you'll be a good leader in Alden's absence."

"Thanks."

Kenji gave him a nod and then went over to Jade. Shona and Jaheem approached him next with grins on their faces.

Jaheem patted him on the back. "Look at you, moving up in the world. After Alden retires, you have a chance of replacing him as captain now that you'll have some experience."

"I agree with Kenji," Shona said. "You'll do great. Just don't overwork us, okay? And don't treat us like we're beneath you now."

"Yeah. Don't let the power go to your head," Jaheem said. "Remember, you're still the baby of the team."

"You guys have nothing to worry about," Kade said reassuringly. "This is temporary."

Jaheem and Shona walked away to check on their dragons. Barret had yet to say anything. He stood there, looking past Kade with a distant gaze. Then he glanced at him and nodded with a blank expression before going to Smoky.

Kade went to Emerald and petted her for a moment. Then he remembered that he needed to give out orders.

"I'll lead the morning patrol." It would give him time to think. "Barret and Shona will come with me. Kenji and Jaheem, take care of the hatchlings and sweep the floor. We also need more terror bird feathers for the nests, although our stock in the storage room is low."

He didn't want to be the captain, but he hoped he wouldn't fail Alden's confidence or his team's trust.

TEN

THE FIRST FEW DAYS went all right, with minimal disruption to the rhythm of the team. After the initial panic, Kade kept reminding himself that Alden would return soon enough, and everything would go back to normal.

One day, Griffin came and looked overjoyed, although she wouldn't tell him what her beaming expression and giggling were about. The only problem was Barret. He spent most of his time brooding.

Kade caught a glare thrown in his direction a few times, and the other rider barely spoke to him. One day, Barret gave an obvious and annoyed sigh when he was told to sweep. Kade sent him on patrol as often as he could to avoid dealing with his teammate's bruised ego.

But on a day when he was stuck with him in the same room, Kade decided to leave the eyrie for a while. Kenji and Jaheem were on patrol. Shona had gone to meet up with Roger.

Kade finished cleaning his saddle and put it back on the rack. "Barret, I'm going out for a while."

The other rider grunted in response.

Kade rolled his eyes. He didn't ask Alden to choose him to be the captain. It would be a relief to get away from the ever-present tension.

He wandered into the stronghold, and it took him a few minutes to find Maysie. She sat at the counter in her shop, examining a pile of gemstones. She wore a blue dress and as much jewelry as last time. Her hair was braided back and held by a rose-shaped hairpin. The shop had wares displayed on the counter, as well as in three wooden cases with glass lids.

Kade patted his clothes where hay was stuck to him and ran his hands through his hair to smooth it down before walking in.

"Maysie?"

She looked up and grinned. "Hi, Kade."

He approached the counter and swallowed nervously, lost for words.

"I was wondering if you would show back up," Maysie said.

"I've been busy. Our captain left a few days ago and put me in charge temporarily."

"Oh, I'm glad you found time to come see me."

Kade stood there for a moment. He hadn't planned any farther than finding Maysie. It was too late in the afternoon to go eat. What could they do?

Maysie looked back down at the gemstones. "So, is this a social visit, or do you want to buy something?"

An idea popped into his head. "Would you like to go outside for a bit? As long as you're not busy."

"No, I'm not busy, and my mom can watch the shop. Let me grab a coat and tell her you're here. I'd like for you to meet her."

"Yes. That would be great."

"Do me a favor and make sure no one steals these." She pointed to the gems.

"No problem."

Maysie went through a door in the back and returned a moment later with an older woman who also had green eyes and curly red hair.

"Kade, this is Odette. Mom, this is Kade."

"Hello, Kade." Odette shook his hand. "You're a dragon rider, right?"

"Yes, ma'am."

She frowned. "I hear that can be a perilous job."

"Every rider knows what they sign up for. It's not much different from being a soldier. We just fight from the back of a dragon."

Odette nodded and smiled, but apprehension showed in her expression.

"Mom, is it all right if we go on a walk?" Maysie asked.

Odette's expression softened. "Sure. Kade, you should come and have supper with us sometime. My husband would like to meet you."

He nodded. "That sounds great."

He and Maysie went to the courtyard outside. The high rampart encircled it, and a great gate reinforced with steel kept any invading army at bay. The dragons would turn any attackers into crisps before they could breach the stronghold, though.

"Maysie, have you ever walked the rampart?"

"The rampart?"

"The wall." He pointed to it.

"No, I haven't. We can do that?"

"I can, and you can come with me." Kade offered her his hand.

She took it, and he turned right and led her up the stairs of the rampart. At the top, she looked around with wonder in her eyes. "This is cool."

As they walked, a soldier here and there stared at them for a moment before recognizing Kade.

"I'm glad that you met my mother," Maysie said. "She's been asking questions about you."

"What kind of questions?"

"Mostly about how safe a dragon rider's job is, but I couldn't say anything on that subject because I had only spoken to you for a few minutes. She was married before to a soldier but only for a year. A troll killed him. She doesn't speak about him often. I don't remember his name."

So that must have been the reason for the apprehension. "I can't promise that I'm safe all the time, but I do everything I can to not be killed."

"That's good because I would worry, too."

They had to squeeze closer together when two soldiers passed by. His body heated up as he made contact with her, despite the chill in the air. They made it to the middle and stopped to look at the landscape.

Several settlements were nearby, the closest one being Dragon's Foot, which was in front of the stronghold. The mountainous landscape extended on to the gray Cloud Spire Mountains. They were so tall that the highest snow-covered peaks were seldom seen.

The air was clearer out here than in the eyrie. Kade took a deep breath and leaned against the battlement. Maysie approached more cautiously. She looked over the edge, and some of the color drained from her face.

"Are you scared of heights?" Kade asked.

"A little." She rested her hands on the battlement. "So, why did you want to become a dragon rider?"

"When I was young, trolls attacked the settlement I lived in. The dragon riders saved us. My father was injured in the attack and asked to be transferred to the stronghold. I became fascinated with dragons and wanted to be a rider to protect people."

"Very heroic. I don't have a story as interesting as that. I've only known the peacefulness of the stronghold for most of my life, learning the names of every gem and how to make jewelry. How long would you remain a rider?"

That question surprised him. He leaned his back on the battlement. "I haven't thought about that. I guess until I'm unable to."

"The job keeps you busy. Are you ever lonely?"

"I have my team and my dragon. And I have you now."

Maysie slid closer and stared at him with affection in her eyes. "Have you thought about having a family?"

"Uh, I need to preferably marry someone before that can happen." Heat rose in his cheeks as she looked him up and down.

"I'd like to have a family before I grow too old. And have a man who will be there for me and protect me." Maysie shivered. "It's cold out here."

Kade wrapped an arm around her. "I can fix that."

She leaned against him and smiled. This felt nice. What would it be like to have a family? To have a wife and children to love and care for?

Maysie looked at him. "Do you have anything you like to do besides working with the dragons?"

"That's a good question. I play cards and chess with my team members, but I haven't taken the time to pursue other hobbies."

"Chess has always been difficult for me to understand. There are too many rules. I do like checkers, and I enjoy reading."

"Excuse me, Captain," someone said behind them.

A royal guard approached and addressed Kade. "The king and queen request your presence in the great hall at once."

Kade turned back to Maysie. "I'm sorry. I was hoping we could stay longer."

"It's all right." Her shoulders slumped. "You need to obey the king and queen."

Kade wrapped his arms around her. "We'll meet up again soon."

Maysie kissed him on the cheek. "It's a date."

Kade felt a rush of excitement that he would see her again. He nodded to the guard. They followed him to the courtyard. In the middle of the staircase, Maysie's foot slipped, and she gasped. Because they were holding hands, Kade swiftly caught her and steadied her, leaning against the railing to keep his balance.

"Are you all right?" he asked.

"Yes, I'm fine. Thank you for catching me. You're such a gentleman," she said.

"You're welcome."

They made it to the courtyard without any more incidents. The gate opened, and mountain goats pulling a wagon came through. The animals were smaller, domesticated versions of their larger cousins in the wild.

Two goblin warriors rode on ponies. They wore green-and-black clothes, and their armor had terror bird motifs. They had curved blades that they called swords strapped to their waists.

"Who's that?" Maysie asked.

Kade frowned and tensed up. "Goblins from Gristnak."

Goblins had green skin in various shades. They denied any relation to trolls. Their ears were longer than dwarf ones. Males grew little hair on their heads and faces. The hair on females barely grew past their shoulders.

Two goblins jumped down from the wagon that was filled with some kind of silvery raw mineral. He didn't know what Drangrere traded with Gristnak.

Soldiers came to speak with the goblins. A few gripped their axes and watched intently. Even though there was peace with Bogden, tension remained between the races.

"Ow. Kade, you're squeezing my hand too tight."

He let her go. "I'm sorry. I didn't mean to."

Maysie rubbed her hand. "I take it you don't like goblins."

"It's complicated." He had been in enough fights with them from Emerald's back, seen what destruction and death they could spread, and they had killed Ada.

"Captain, the king and queen await," the guard said.

Kade pulled himself out of his suspicious staring. "Yes. I'm sorry. Maysie, would you like me to walk you back to your shop?"

"No, I'll be fine. You can go ahead."

"I'll see you soon." A comfortable warmth filled his chest.

Maysie gave him a soft smile. "I'm looking forward to it."

Kade followed the guard and watched Maysie walk away until he couldn't see her.

ELEVEN

Kade strode into the great hall. Skylights on the ceiling and braziers on the floor illuminated the large room. Columns, which had been richly sculpted, lined each side. Large banners and murals adorned the walls, one painting being of Sapphire and Moonstone in flight. There were still spaces for more significant events to be memorialized.

King Magus sat upon the dragon bone throne. It was constructed entirely of bones, talons, and teeth, with patterns of dragons carved into them. The hilts on the royals' weapons were made from the same materials. Queen Helga stood on the left side of the throne, and Griffin was on the right. The princess had a big grin on her face and looked as if she was nearly bouncing in place with excitement that she could barely contain. Kade stopped at the steps that led up to the throne and bowed.

"I summoned you because my daughter once again requested to ride a dragon," Magus said, "something we have always denied without question."

Based on Griffin's joyful mood, Kade was about to be asked for a favor.

"But with her wedding and move to Carodhall approaching, her mother and I," he gave a cautious glance at Helga, "believe that one time will be all right."

Helga nodded, but her face was tense.

"Of course, we want to ensure that Griffin will be as safe as possible."

"Your graces, I will take the princess out myself and bring her back unharmed. I promise that nothing horrible will happen to her." He hoped he knew what he was agreeing to.

"Thank you, Kade," Helga said.

"When is the best time to go out?" Magus asked.

"The weather has been fair. In the past few days, attacks have lessened. They usually take place in the evening or at night. I can take the princess out tomorrow morning. I'll leave Barret in charge while I'm gone." That might make the other rider happy for a few hours.

Magus stood. "Griffin will see you in the morning, then."

The king and queen left, and Griffin bounded up to Kade.

"Isn't this great? I've been wanting this for so long."

Kade rubbed the back of his neck. "As long as it won't end with me being executed," he muttered.

"What?"

"Nothing. Come as early as you can. You'll need pants, boots, and gloves. Dress warmly and wear a chain mail shirt and armor. The necklace could fly off, so leave it behind." This was going to be a huge mistake, wasn't it?

Griffin hugged him tightly. "Thank you for agreeing to let me do this. It's a dream come true."

TWELVE

GRIFFIN HAD TO FORCE herself not to run to the eyrie. The sun had barely risen, and the air was chilly when she went through the skywalk. A thick fog lay in the valley, but the sky was clear. She had hardly slept and had gulped her breakfast down. As far as Griffin knew, the riders hadn't gone out last night, so Kade and Emerald should be well rested. She had no guard with her because it hadn't seemed necessary.

She had worn what Kade had suggested. Comfortable boots, woolen silver pants, a blue fur-lined coat over a woolen gray tunic, thick black gloves, a chain mail shirt, and a few pieces of her armor. But she carried the helmet for the moment. She also brought a blue scarf and carried a dagger and a small throwing axe. Kade would bring weapons as well, so Griffin didn't think she needed anything else. It was just a joy ride. They shouldn't encounter any trouble, right?

The door to the eyrie wasn't open yet. She was the first one here. Griffin knocked three times, as Alden had instructed and pressed her ear to the door.

This gave the dragons time if some of them were otherwise occupied. There was no noise, so Griffin opened the door. It could be locked but rarely was. Someone would have to be crazy to go into a room with dragons and start trouble.

The eyrie was warmer. All of the dragons slept in their nests. Emerald opened her eyes and glanced warmly at Griffin. Then she yawned and curled up tighter in her nest. Ruby gave a friendly rumble as Griffin passed by her. She rubbed the red dragon on her head and looked over at Crystal.

The white dragon had woken and stared at her. Griffin went over to her, having to walk around Smoky's tail, and sat by Crystal's head, which was resting on the floor. The dragon's eyes were clearer and more alert today, instead of being clouded by a haze of grief. Griffin rubbed her head. She stopped petting, and Crystal bumped her legs with her snout, as though demanding more attention.

"All right. I won't stop." Griffin giggled. She grabbed a stool so she wouldn't have to sit on the cold floor.

Topaz opened his light blue eyes and watched for a moment before going back to sleep.

Griffin petted Crystal again. "One day, you'll remember Ada without feeling sad. She loved you so much, and I know you adored her. Her death isn't your fault. Your next rider will be lucky to have you as their mount. Can I tell you a secret?"

Crystal gave a rumble. Griffin checked the door and then leaned closer.

"I wish it was me. But we have to accept that we are bound by duties thrust upon us since birth. Sometimes they can be changed, but otherwise, it's just the way life is."

Griffin heard footsteps. Kade walked through the door. He stared at her in surprise, and then he grinned. "I won the bet."

Griffin tilted her head. "You guys made a bet on me?"

"Yep. On when you would arrive. I'm the only one who said you'd beat all of us to the eyrie."

Griffin stood and straightened out her clothes. "I don't know whether to be flattered or offended."

Kade shrugged. "It was all in good fun."

"Fun is what I hope today will be. I barely slept. I was so excited. When will we be leaving?"

Kade yawned and blinked sleepily. "Give me a few minutes to get ready and collect my earnings."

While waiting for her friend, Griffin gave the other dragons attention. Even grumpy Jade couldn't resist a good chin scratching. The other riders arrived, and the big doors were opened, letting sunshine and cool air drift into the eyrie. The fog had lifted outside.

This was it. She was minutes away. Her heart beat faster, and her stomach felt unsettled. But this wasn't the time for nerves to make her sick. She took a few calming breaths as she watched Kade and Jaheem haul the double-saddle and the bags onto Emerald's back. Then they slipped a single-headed and a double-headed axe into sheaths on either side of the saddle.

Shona handed her a pair of goggles. "Do you know how to wrap the scarf around your head, Princess?"

"Yeah, I can get it."

Before she could start, Kade walked up to her with a harness.

"I'm sure you already know, but buckle the long strap around your waist. Tighten it enough to be comfortable. The short straps go around your legs." She finished with that and then stepped toward the dragon.

"Griffin, the headgear. It's going to be cold."

"Right. Yes." Griffin retrieved the forgotten equipment from the floor. "This stuff will mess up my hair." She had braided it into a beautiful bun that might get pulled loose.

Kade tilted his head. "And the wind won't?"

Yeah. He had her there. "Oh, all right."

It took a couple of times to wrap the scarf correctly, but she got everything on comfortably. Now it was time. Her body seemed to vibrate as they went to Emerald's right side.

"Let me go first," Kade said, his voice a little muffled by his scarf. He stepped onto Emerald's wing and climbed into the saddle.

At a nod from him, Griffin put her left foot on the dragon's wing. She was aware of the other riders watching as she mounted more slowly and carefully. Kade held a hand out, which she gladly took to help her climb into the saddle behind him.

"This is the first time we've used the double-saddle since I've been a rider," he said.

It wasn't much larger than a regular saddle. The seat extended out enough for two dwarves to sit comfortably. "Clip the straps hanging from your harness to the rings on either side."

With that done, it hit her. She was on a dragon. It felt like all the dreams she'd had of this moment.

"What do I do now, Kade?"

"Wrap your arms around me, and move with Emerald. When she goes left, lean left. When she goes right, lean right. Lean forward for up and down. If she goes upside down, hang on for dear life. Fly, Emerald."

The dragon stood. Griffin was lost in her thoughts and was shifted off balance for a second. Keeping her seat was more difficult than when riding a pony. She held onto Kade and attempted to move with Emerald to stay balanced. The dragon went to the drop-off and took a huge breath. Then, with a roar, she leaped out of the eyrie and spread her wings.

Thirteen

GRIFFIN DIDN'T EXPECT THE lightheaded feeling and as if her stomach dropped as Emerald fell a little distance. Then the dragon flapped her wings and ascended. The wind rushed past her, and she saw the landscape from a height she could only imagine before. It was breathtaking.

Joy flooded through her body. Emerald turning left unbalanced her again. She needed to focus on the dragon's movements. Kade's, too, for that matter. When he leaned one way or the other, that signaled his mount to turn.

He had Emerald circle over the stronghold so she could see it from above. From all angles, her home looked impressive. In the sun's light, the Blood Spear Mountains had a reddish glow from the foothills to the peaks. She could fully appreciate the view from the sky. Then they turned away from the stronghold and flew toward the Cloud Spire Mountains. Emerald passed over the lower peaks.

Griffin knew the world was large, but from the back of a dragon, it stretched on infinitely. Emerald effortlessly flew over valleys, hills, and mountains that would take days to cross on foot or on ponyback. Cold air rushed past her but was mostly repelled by her armor and warm clothes.

Emerald ascended higher into the clouds, and Griffin had to wipe moisture from her goggles. She pushed down a wave of panic at being so far from the ground. The safety straps would keep her from falling. They glided above the clouds for a bit and then descended back below them. Kade wasn't directing Emerald, just letting his mount have fun.

Griffin let go of Kade and held her arms out, feeling as if she was flying. Then the dragon steeply dived. Griffin grabbed hold of Kade again with a gasp. She felt and heard him chuckle. Emerald went through a valley, buffeting the trees in her wake. A flock of frightened doves ascended from the forest.

"Duck!" Kade yelled.

Griffin leaned forward. A few of the birds passed over them. Wings fluttered near Griffin's head, and a ding sounded against her helmet. Kade sat back up and turned to look at her. She couldn't see his mouth, but from his eyes, she could tell he was grinning.

"Are you having fun?" he asked.

"Very much so."

She eventually got used to Emerald's movements. Once she paid attention, it wasn't too hard to anticipate where the dragon would go next. Her head pointed in the direction first before her body followed, as well as other subtle cues. After a while, Griffin wasn't sure if she recognized the landscape below them.

"Kade, where are we?"

He looked on either side. "Flying along the southern border." He pointed to the right. "That's the Dragon's Tail Mountains over there."

That range separated Drangrere from the goblin kingdoms with a wide stretch of wild lands on both sides. It stretched out in a line that went east as far as Carodhall. Some peaks reached high enough to have snow on them. The mountains were dark gray, almost black in places.

Something let out a terrible screech behind them, followed by several more. Emerald looked back and growled. Griffin and Kade also checked. Four terror birds were chasing them.

FOURTEEN

T HE BIRDS GAINED ON them, letting out frightening shrieks from their large curved beaks that made Griffin want to cover her ears. Kade pulled the double-headed axe out and slipped his hand through the leather loop on the haft. She would pull a weapon out too, but she was scared to let go of Kade.

"Keep your head down and hang on," he said. "Emerald, fly fast."

His dragon folded her wings and descended. The wind rushed past Griffin's head so loudly, she could barely hear. Emerald gained some ground, but the terror birds relentlessly chased her. They could be territorial and aggressive, bold enough to attack a dragon twice their size. It was like when mockingbirds chased a hawk or an owl.

Out of nowhere, two black shapes appeared from underneath them. Emerald roared and turned to the south. Griffin saw the brown underside of one bird as it flew over them, its talons extending to grab them. The story of the doomed dragon rider prince flashed in her mind.

Griffin screamed as up suddenly became down. Emerald twisted around and swiped at the terror bird with a back foot. Griffin squeezed her legs against the saddle and closed her eyes as they plummeted through the air for a moment. She heard and felt Emerald breathe fire, and then the dragon righted herself. When Griffin opened her eyes and looked over her shoulder, the terror birds had flown around the fireball and were still in pursuit.

Her heart beat faster, and she clung to Kade. Emerald couldn't fight all the terror birds and protect her riders alone. And now they were going away from Drangrere, farther into the wilderness. The dragon put on a burst of speed again and zoomed around rock formations and into a canyon. It curved up ahead, and Emerald took it as fast as she could, leaving the terror birds behind. The canyon opened into a valley that had a forest with a large lake in the center.

Kade pointed with his axe to a ledge on the cliff wall to the right. "Land there."

The dragon swiftly turned and dropped onto the ledge. It held. Rocks on the edge made a natural wall like a parapet.

"Emerald, lie down."

Griffin had no idea how Kade was so calm. She was shaking, and she could barely think. Although, the shivering might also be because the cold air was seeping through as a result of the speedy flight.

"Head down, girl," Kade said. The dragon obeyed. "Griffin, lean forward."

She ducked as the terror birds screeched again. Griffin heard the beats of their wings as they flew into the valley. They screamed again but in a high-pitched and fearful tone. Those creatures weren't scared of anything. What did they see?

A thunderous roar echoed through the valley. Griffin lifted her head and gasped. A massive, golden-scaled dragon was perched on a precipice to the right. Emerald growled.

"Easy, Em. Quiet," Kade commanded.

The wild dragon roared again and leaped into the air in pursuit of the terror birds. It was two to three times the size of Emerald, and its golden scales glittered in the sunlight. One terror bird turned to face the dragon. Its shriek was cut off by the fireball that enveloped it. Griffin winced. The dragon snatched the toasted body out of the sky and swallowed it in three chomps.

Griffin remembered a conversation the riders had had recently. "Kade, is that Syrene? The one I've heard you guys talk about?"

"Yeah, that's her. This is my first time seeing her. Alden, Barret, and Shona have. Now I can add my name to the list."

Syrene was the largest female dragon that they knew of, named after the goddess, Syrene, the Lady of Gold.

Kade checked the surrounding skies. "I don't know where her mate is. He's bigger than her."

"What color is he?"

"Silver. That's why he was named after the god, Zallar, the Warrior of Iron. He'd have to be a warrior to have survived and grown to be the largest male dragon in the region. It's weird, though."

"Why?"

"I didn't realize they were close to Drangrere. I doubt that, even with the entire team, we'd be able to chase them away if they crossed the border."

After seeing Syrene, it was a wonder that dragons were ever tamed. They would probably always have a little wild in them, but they wouldn't have the ferociousness of one not born in captivity.

"I know one thing." Kade said as he glanced around and sheathed his axe. "I want to leave before Syrene comes back. Her nest must be nearby. We'll start heading back to the stronghold."

"As long as we take the scenic route, that's fine with me."

"Emerald, fly."

FIFTEEN

E MERALD FLEW BACK THROUGH the canyon. This time, Griffin could admire the natural features around her. The walls of the canyon had different colors and layers of stone. She'd never see it like this from the ground. They emerged and encountered angry storm clouds on the northern horizon that blocked the way back to the stronghold.

"Wait, Em," Kade commanded. The dragon hovered in place. He turned his head. "We'll have to go around the storm, or at least wait for it to pass. We have to head west, but we need to be careful to avoid Raggerath. I don't feel like starting a one-man war with Nafrag today."

"It's okay. I trust you."

Kade leaned left. They flew far enough past the storm that they seemed to be out of its path.

He turned to Griffin again. "Want to take a break?"

As much as she didn't want to, her butt was getting numb from sitting for so long, and she wouldn't mind a break from the cold wind. "Sure."

Kade directed Emerald toward a narrow valley. It was mostly rocky, with sparse trees and vegetation.

The stone was more of a tan color. The dragon landed by a gentle stream that flowed out from the side of a mountain.

Dismounting the dragon was easier than mounting. All Griffin had to do was step onto Emerald's wing and hop down when she was low enough. She pulled the helmet off, lowered the goggles to hang around her neck, and pulled the scarf down from her mouth. Emerald got a long drink from the stream. Griffin took in a deep breath and checked on how her hairdo was holding. Then she walked a little distance away.

"Griffin, we're in wild lands right now," Kade said. "Be careful."

"I'm always careful," she said, rolling her eyes when Kade couldn't see her face. Rocks tumbled, and she paused. Her eyes darted around as she searched for where the sound came from. Then she sighed in relief.

A herd of ibexes was climbing the valley slope. The animals nimbly picked their way up the rocks, even when their path was nearly vertical. She never understood how they could do that. Goblins had similar climbing skills, but dwarves were too stout and stocky.

Griffin went back to Kade and Emerald. "By the way, how are things going with Maysie? Did you see her again?"

He smiled shyly. "Yeah."

"Do you like her?"

"Yes. I'm planning to see her again as soon as I can."

"Good." Griffin was glad that her friend was happy. He deserved it.

They took time to eat, drink, and rest. Griffin was jealous that Kade could fly to places like this and enjoy time out in the wild. For once, she didn't have to worry about duties or behaving like a princess or making sure her guard didn't fall behind. Out here was freedom, and besides terror birds, wild dragons, and trolls, there was peace. Except for the second strange noises she just heard, like a grunt and something large plodding across stone. That was no ibex. Was it a bear or worse?

Kade furrowed his brow and unsheathed the double-headed axe again. "Stay here."

"No way. I want to see, too."

"Then stay close to me."

Emerald followed, as well.

Kade donned his helmet but left the goggles hanging around his neck. Griffin did the same. The valley curved to the left, and then there was a cliff. They walked to the edge and looked over. Griffin gasped.

Speaking of trolls, there were several below them. Kade pulled her back and put a finger to his lips. She nodded. Emerald sniffed the air and growled.

"Hush, girl," Kade said.

He crept to the edge again. Never mind about the wilderness being entirely peaceful. This was terrifying but also a little exciting. Kade beckoned to her, and she joined him at the cliff.

There were seven trolls, including a young one. They traveled across a ledge far below. Griffin had never seen a troll. Being confined to the stronghold for most of her life and only traveling in safe areas prevented encounters like this. Her parents would be furious if she told them. Some trolls carried stone weapons, one had a wooden club, and one had a poleaxe that it must have stolen from a dwarf soldier. It was difficult to tell which ones were male or female. Their bodies looked too similar.

"I kind of feel bad for them," Griffin said.

Kade tilted his head.

"They're just creatures trying to survive. We're moving into their home and pushing them out. Then they get angry and try to chase us away. If they wouldn't attack us, there'd be no reason to kill them."

Kade pursed his lips. "There's nothing that can be done about it. We can't communicate with them and tell them why we're expanding into their territories. And we have the right to defend ourselves."

"They also have that right. It doesn't seem fair. Who are the bad guys in that situation?"

Kade shrugged. "If it makes you feel better, on the troll attack calls, some of them have the good sense to run when they see the dragons. We don't always have to kill all of them."

Emerald growled again.

"Em, be quiet," Kade said.

But she growled louder and turned around. Two trolls had snuck up on them while they were distracted. Oh, no. Oh, no. Oh, no. Griffin backed away but forgot about the cliff. She gasped when her right heel stepped over the edge, and Kade grabbed her arm as she lurched forward. Then he held his axe at the ready.

"Will that do anything?" Griffin asked.

"No. We need to get back on Emerald."

Griffin pulled her throwing axe out, even though the weapon would be even more useless. The dragon reared her head back to breathe fire. One troll threw a club at her, hitting her neck and interrupting the process. She roared angrily at it. Kade and Griffin made it to her side, but then she lunged at the troll, leaving them exposed.

They both shared wide-eyed expressions as the other troll took the opening. It carried a familiar-looking dwarf spear and had a healing wound on its left shoulder that was partially visible at the edge of its fur pelt shirt. The troll had short, black hair. It narrowed its eyes and growled at them.

"Kade, is that the troll you didn't kill at Hoeckan?"

"Yeah. And I think it's angry with me."

They leaped apart as Kade's troll thrust the spear down with a roar of rage. Griffin screamed and fell to the ground. The troll loomed over her, and she froze. She felt as if she couldn't breathe. Today wasn't supposed to go like this. Emerald raced back, and the troll ran and ducked when she let out a stream of fire.

"Griffin!" Kade yelled.

She stood with shaky legs. Her heart was beating so hard she thought it would explode. Griffin ran to Kade. A third troll came around the corner. Emerald couldn't keep all of them at bay.

Kade grabbed her hand. "Come on. We have to climb."

The wall of the valley wasn't as steep here. If they got high enough, Emerald could fly up to them. Behind them, the dragon breathed fire again, and a troll screamed. Kade led the way up the slope. How was he so calm? He hadn't been able to talk to a girl without her pushing him into it.

There was a roar behind them, and a troll ran up the slope toward them. It had a stone weapon that had been fashioned into an axe. The brute nimbly traversed the slope, able to step across large boulders that Griffin and Kade weren't tall enough to climb. They would never outrun it.

Kade opened his mouth to call for Emerald, but as they backed up, Griffin's feet stepped into nothingness.

SIXTEEN

THE LANDING KNOCKED THE wind out of her body and the axe out of her hand, but the floor was sandy. It took a moment to get her bearings and recover. Sand flying tickled her nose, and she held back a sneeze. Her head had hit the floor, but the helmet took the brunt of the impact. Kade groaned next to her.

"Are you okay?" she asked.

"Yeah."

"The helmet was a good idea, after all."

"Yeah. Armor can be useful."

The face of the troll appeared in the hole. It growled and reached a hand toward them. Griffin and Kade scrambled away. She screamed as fingers grasped for her.

"Get away from her!" Kade swung his axe at the troll's hand, slicing a gash across the back of it.

Griffin slashed one of its fingers with her axe. The troll screamed and withdrew. Griffin and Kade ran down a tunnel into the darkness as they heard the troll slipping through the hole.

"What do we do now?" Griffin asked in a trembling voice.

"Find a way out and call for Emerald," Kade said, calm as ever, as if this was routine for him. She guessed it kind of was.

He grabbed her hand again. Tears welled in her eyes. She'd had enough adventure for today. She wanted to go home and cuddle Sir Whiskers in the safety of her bedroom. There was a loud thud behind them. The troll must have gotten through.

They kept running. Narrow shafts of sunlight from cracks and holes pierced the darkness of the tunnels. Kade abruptly turned down a side passage.

They followed it until it ended in a cave. There was a hole higher up with a few rocks piled up underneath. It looked like they could fit through, but the troll wouldn't be able to. Griffin sheathed her axe and climbed up the rocks, but she couldn't reach the edge of the hole. Zallar and Syrene, help them.

"Maybe I can lift you out," Kade said.

"But I may not be able to pull you up."

He glanced at the tunnel and then gripped his bloodied axe tightly. "You're the princess. My duty is to protect you."

Griffin stared at him with wide eyes. "But you're my friend. Your life is important to me, too."

"You go and find Emerald. There may be enough time before it finds me."

She shook her head. "No. I'm not leaving you. We're both getting out. That's an order from your princess."

"Yes, my lady." He still looked unsure.

A roar echoed through the tunnel. The troll was catching up. But a high-pitched roar answered it. Then there was the sound of fighting, screams, and large bodies being thrown against walls. Something else caught her attention. Various animal bones were piled up in two corners of the cave. Kade noticed, too. The sour tang of decay hung in the air. What creature's home had they fallen into? The fighting raged on.

Kade pushed her toward the hole. "We have to get out now."

Griffin climbed up the rock pile again. Kade put her on his shoulders to lift her higher.

She scrabbled for the edge. "I can't reach."

"Keep trying."

Griffin reached as far as she could, her sides protesting at being overstretched. Almost there. Her fingers touched the edge. Then Kade lost his balance, and they both fell. Griffin slid off his back so she wouldn't fall on him.

She climbed the rocks as close to the hole as she could. "Emerald!"

"Shhh. Griffin, do you want those things to find us?"

Yeah. Maybe yelling where they were trapped with a troll and an unknown creature was stupid, but she was scared. "Sorry."

There was a pained scream, probably from the troll, and then silence fell. Kade and Griffin stood still. Outside, something large thudded against the ground, and rocks clattered and tumbled.

A green-scaled snout appeared at the hole and sniffed.

"Emerald, we're here," Kade said with a grin.

Relief rushed through Griffin. The dragon turned her head to look in the hole with one eye.

Kade and Griffin climbed up the rock pile. Then a deep growl echoed through the tunnel, and heavy footsteps stomped toward them.

"Emerald, pull us out," Kade said. "Give me a foot."

The dragon reached a wing foot through the hole. Kade indicated for Griffin to go first. She grabbed the foot and held on as Emerald lifted her out. Then Griffin looked back into the cave. The creature had come close enough that she could make out eyeshine and an outline in the shadows of the tunnel. It was a large, hairy animal that walked on two legs and had horns on its head.

Emerald growled and then breathed in. Griffin squeezed her hands under her helmet to cover her ears before the dragon roared. The creature backed off, and Emerald pulled Kade out. They were safe.

SEVENTEEN

K ADE LEANED ON HIS axe and waited for his ears to stop ringing from Emerald's roar. They were on the other side of the valley, and there were no trolls in sight. He breathed in the fresh mountain air. This was much better than being trapped in the confines of a cave with a creature he had never seen before. He glanced at the hole, but nothing appeared in it.

Emerald must have scared the creature away. Griffin had been right to yell for her. That was the most frightening experience he had ever had as a dragon rider, mostly because he was cut off from Emerald. Riders were trained to fight, but their greatest weapons were their dragons.

Griffin had sat and held her head in her hands. What would the queen and king say if they heard about their daughter's misadventures? Thunder rumbled in the distance.

Emerald came to him and nuzzled his chest. He petted her. "It's okay, girl. We're all right."

Kade checked her for injuries, but she was unharmed. Then the dragon let out an excited squeal and went to inspect some glittery rocks. Kade walked over to Griffin, who hadn't moved.

"Griffin?"

She lifted her head and had glassy eyes and a strained expression on her face. Her skin looked paler. "After all the fight training that I've received, I imagined that I'd know what to do if I needed to use those skills. But I couldn't stop panicking. Even if I had the chance to be a dragon rider, I may not be cut out for the job."

Kade chuckled.

Griffin glared. "Don't laugh at me."

"I'm sorry. I'm not laughing at you. This is your first flight and your first fights. When you're a rider, you go out the first time, get the crap scared out of you, go to sleep thinking you can never do it again, and then climb into the saddle the next day. And once that happens a dozen more times, you get used to it. It's like riding a pony."

"Was it like that for you? Is that why you're so calm?"

"I'm not immune to feeling scared. This many bad things didn't happen on my first flight, though. A terror bird attacked me, but Onyx chased it away."

After a moment, Griffin relaxed her posture. "Speaking of Onyx, have you heard anything about where Alden is?"

Kade shook his head. "I don't know where he went. There's been no recent reports of them being sighted."

Emerald came to Griffin and nuzzled her, too. She wrapped her arms around the dragon's snout and kissed it. "Thank you for saving us."

Kade held a hand out and helped her up. "I know we almost got eaten by a...whatever that thing was, but we made it out. And you live to ride another day. That's what it means to be a dragon rider."

Griffin nodded and gave a small smile. "Still, I'm ready to go home." She looked over his shoulder and frowned. "The storm's close."

Thunder rumbled louder, and the wind picked up. The storm clouds had grown larger and were now heading toward them.

"I hope we can get around that," Kade said as he studied the clouds. He didn't want to fly through it.

"Hey, Kade, look," Griffin said. He turned back around, and she held a gold coin in her hand that had a dragon inscribed on it. The face on the other side was too damaged to see who the royal was. "I've heard about finding coins out in the middle of nowhere from cargo that wild dragons have stolen. This is my first one."

"They're supposed to bring good luck."

She held it out to him. "You can have it. You're my good luck."

Kade hesitated. "Are you sure?"

"Take it before I change my mind."

"Thanks, Griffin." He pocketed the coin. It was too damaged to be spent, so it would be added to his collection at home.

Kade positioned Emerald by some rocks so they could climb onto her easier. They mounted up and cleaned the axes. Please, Syrene and Zallar, let there be no more trouble. Kade sheathed his axe back on the saddle.

"To the eyrie, Emerald. Go around the storm."

The dragon leaped into the air, and they were safely back in the sky. They had to fly farther through the wilderness and skirt the edge of Bogden's kingdom, Gristnak. Kade stayed watchful for terror birds and wild dragons. With the storm approaching, those creatures should hunker down, which would be lucky for him and Griffin.

Dragon's Talons Ridge was coming up. The peaks were pointier and lower than the Dragon's Tail and separated Gristnak from Raggerath. They would not want to cross them into Nafrag's kingdom. He checked the storm clouds. They might get wet, but they couldn't go any farther west. Emerald hadn't turned yet, so Kade leaned right. Griffin tapped his shoulder.

"Is that a dragon?" she asked and pointed to a large, dark shape spread out on the ground in a valley on the Gristnak side of the Talons.

It looked like a dragon, but it wasn't moving.

"Emerald." Kade pointed toward the shape.

She saw it and circled down. It was a dragon. A black one. And did it have a saddle? Kade's heart dropped, and for the first time in a long time as a rider, he froze. A smaller shape lay next to the dragon.

No. Please, no. Let it not be them.

EIGHTEEN

H E HARDLY ACKNOWLEDGED EMERALD landing. Kade felt as if he could barely breathe, and his body seemed numb. This couldn't be real. Griffin was unclipping herself, and Kade broke out of his shock to do the same.

She put a hand on his shoulder and gave him a sympathetic look. With great reluctance, he dismounted. The scarf felt as though it was suffocating him, so he pulled everything off his head. But that gave him little comfort.

In a gray, stony valley next to a pale blue lake lay Onyx. She was at an odd angle, as if she had fallen out of the sky. Dried blood made a pool of red around her. Her eyes were closed, and two ballista bolts with black fletching stuck out of her chest.

On her other side was Alden. Kade ran to him. The captain also lay still with his eyes closed. Unsurprisingly, he wasn't wearing his cuirass. Alden had spoken often about it being uncomfortable to wear for hours. Two large crossbow bolts with orange fletching had pierced the chain mail and protruded from his chest.

The clips on the safety straps were broken, probably from the force of the fall. Kade checked for a pulse with a flicker of hope that maybe his captain was alive. Alden's skin was pale and cold, and no pulse thumped at his neck.

Tears stung his eyes. Emerald sniffed Onyx and then let out a mournful cry. Kade sat on a rock as his legs felt weak. How did this happen? What was Alden doing so far from dwarf lands? Thunder rumbled in the distance. Kade checked on Griffin. She stood nearby, wiping away tears that streamed down her face.

The cry of a terror bird startled him. Three of them circled overhead. He ran to Emerald and pulled the double-headed axe off the saddle again. The birds wouldn't feast on Alden and Onyx if he could help it. Emerald waited for a command.

Griffin joined him. "Kade, look. Do they have riders?"

She was right. The terror birds descending toward them wore saddles, and goblins rode on their backs. One landed near them, squawking as it slipped on loose rocks. The rider was thrown forward and had to hang onto the saddle.

"We need to work on your landings, Fasta," the goblin said. "Let me down, girl."

Fasta crouched to let him dismount. The goblin pulled his goggles down and then lowered the green scarf that was wrapped around his head to uncover his mouth. He unclipped straps from a saddle that was similar to dragon ones. The other two riders stayed on their mounts. They were goblins of Gristnak.

Emerald growled and then roared. Fasta fluffed her feathers up to look larger and shrieked back.

"Easy," Kade told his dragon, even as he clutched his axe.

The goblin stroked the terror bird's neck and then came up to them. He had one blue eye and one brown eye. Each eye being a different color was common in goblins.

"Greetings," the goblin said kindly. "My name is Riggs. I'm the commander of the terror bird riders. I would ask what brings a dragon rider and his companion to Gristnak, but the answer's obvious." Riggs's facial structure was more angular. He had a crossbow strapped to his back and a sword and a dagger at his waist. Commander was their equivalent of a captain.

Griffin stepped forward. "I am Princess Griffin of Drangrere." Her voice was a little shaky. "And Kade was taking me on a joyride when we ran into some trouble and happened across this."

"My Lady." Riggs bowed. "I thought dragons were nearly invincible."

"Do you know what happened?" Kade asked curtly.

"No one witnessed the act, but let me see here." Riggs looked Onyx and Alden over. "Nafrag has ballistae set up on the other side of the Talons, as well as crossbowmen high on the slopes, to shoot my riders down. We use green fletching, so I assume the dragon flew too low, was shot, and at some point, the rider was hit by two crossbow bolts. Then, while escaping the danger, they both fell on our side of the Talons. It must have happened only a day or two ago. I can assure you both that we would never kill a dragon rider. Lord Bogden has no intention of breaking the truce between our people and the dwarves."

Riggs kneeled next to Alden and broke off the end of one of the crossbow bolts. Then he clasped his hands together and bowed his head in respect to the fallen rider.

"Was flying over goblin lands part of Alden's plans?" Griffin muttered to Kade.

"No. I don't know why he was out here." He loosened his grip on his axe and leaned on it as a wave of grief flooded through him again. The weapon was the only thing helping him stay upright.

He jumped at a crack of thunder. The storm was barreling toward them. A gust of cool wind carried the sweet smell of rain.

Riggs approached. He halted when Emerald let out a soft growl. "You both should come to our stronghold to wait out the storm."

"We'll be leaving to inform the king about my captain's death," Kade said brusquely.

Griffin shot him a look. "We need to make arrangements for what will be done with the bodies, especially because they're not in Drangrere. Commander, we will come with you and wait for the storm to pass before returning home. I will be honored to speak with Lord Bogden."

Riggs bowed his head. Kade pursed his lips and stared at his boots. Griffin was better at diplomacy.

"Follow us," the goblin said, and then he looked at Emerald apprehensively. "And don't let the dragon eat our birds."

Griffin and Kade mounted back up. He sighed as he donned his helmet. "Emerald," he couldn't believe he was about to say this, "follow the terror birds."

She obeyed and trailed after the goblins.

Nineteen

K ADE HAD NEVER BEEN this far into Gristnak before. They passed over a few scattered settlements. The stronghold wasn't far from the Talons. The Evergreen Mountains rose up behind it. They were named for their patches of green-and-black granite and the abundant evergreen trees on their slopes. Kade smelled the sharp, earthy scent as they approached.

A great gate was set at the foot of the mountains along with a thick stone rampart. Granite terror bird statues perched on the edges of the battlement like gargoyles. The craftsmanship was as skilled as what dwarves could build.

They flew over the rampart and through a hole in a mountain that led to a courtyard inside. Goblins paused and watched as a dragon landed in their home. Kade and Griffin dismounted, and Riggs approached as his terror bird followed the other two back through the hole. A warrior walked up to them.

"Nial," Riggs said, "tell his grace that he has visitors from Drangrere."

"Yes, Commander." Nial nodded and left.

Tall columns made from green-and-black granite spanned across the stronghold entrance, but the spaces were too narrow for Emerald to squeeze through.

"Your dragon can rest there." Riggs pointed out a nook at one end of the columns, where she would be out of the way and sheltered from the rain. With his scarf off, Kade saw that the goblin had short, black hair.

"Come on, girl," Kade said and led her to that spot. "Stay here."

As she settled down, some goblins stared at her in amazement, wonder, or curiosity. But there were also glares and suspicious expressions thrown their way.

Riggs spoke to a few warriors, who then came to stand around Emerald. "These goblins will guard her," he said. The warriors cast worried looks at Emerald, who had put her head down and closed her eyes. "We'll see the king now."

Griffin was unusually subdued and quiet with a frown on her face.

"Are you okay?" Kade asked.

"I'm a princess. I have to be okay. But today's been a tough day."

They left their headgear with Emerald and followed Riggs through the halls of the stronghold. Kade was impressed. The architecture was expertly crafted and carved, but also with a roughness, as though the goblins were preserving the natural textures of the mountains.

Hallways stretched on endlessly, and the stronghold was as much of a maze and as bustling with citizens as a dwarf one. They entered the great hall, which was more like a large cave chamber lit with torches and braziers. Kade heard a faint rumble of thunder.

Bogden sat on a throne of granite carved into the shape of a terror bird. The feet were the armrests, the head loomed over the top, and the wings spread out from the sides. The king was a burly goblin with dark green skin, wispy gray hair, and brown eyes. He wore a green long-sleeved doublet that was richly embroidered and dark green pants. Several rings adorned his fingers, and a gold crown with green gemstones sat upon his head.

Riggs bowed. "My king, I present Princess Griffin of Drangrere and her companion, a dragon rider. What was his name again?"

"Kade," Griffin said after he hesitated.

Kade looked away for a second, and then a hand tapped his side. He was supposed to be bowing. Kade lowered his head.

Griffin stepped closer. "My lord Bogden, thank you for allowing us to shelter in your home until the storm has passed. My father will be pleased to hear about the hospitality you have shown us."

"The pleasure is mine, Princess," he said with a smile and inclined his head. "Magus has been a wonderful ally, and any of his family or his people are always welcome here in Gristnak. I heard there was some trouble on my lands."

"Yes," Griffin said sadly. "Nafrag's goblins shot down one of our dragons, Onyx, and killed the captain of the dragon riders, Alden."

"Here's proof." Riggs handed the king the crossbow bolt piece.

Anger flashed in Bogden's eyes. "Taking potshots at my riders is one thing. Those goblins are either bold or idiotic to shoot down a dragon rider. Where are the bodies?"

"On the western edge of the kingdom by the Ice Blue Lake."

Bogden tapped his fingers on the armrest. "I don't know what you want to do with Onyx's body, but what of Alden's remains, Princess?"

She looked at Kade. "I'm not the one to make the final decision about Alden, and I assume Onyx's body will have to stay."

Kade nodded. Considering the distance, safely moving a dragon of her size was impossible, and he needed to speak with his team about Alden.

"Emery," Bogden said to a well-dressed goblin standing nearby, "after the storm passes, take warriors and a couple of terror birds to guard the bodies so scavengers don't defile them."

"Yes, Father," the goblin said. He had short brown hair and a stubble beard. His one brown eye and one blue eye were both narrowed as he stared at Griffin and Kade. Clearly, not everyone in the royal family trusted dwarves.

"Also, go tell your mother that we have guests."

Emery nodded and left through a side door. Kade thought he caught a scowl on the goblin's face.

Bogden rubbed his chin. "I am curious what a dragon rider was doing flying over goblin lands alone."

"He meant no threat to you. I can assure you of that," Griffin said. "He was on an extended patrol to observe and assess our borders for threats. Commander Riggs believes he flew too close to Raggerath. Something must have caught his attention."

The king nodded. Then he tilted his head and furrowed his eyebrows. "And what are you doing out here? When last I checked, royals don't ride dragons."

"Kade was giving me a joy ride, a gift for my upcoming wedding."

"And does the rider concur with this, or does he not speak?"

Griffin nodded to Kade.

He cleared his throat as he fought down reluctance to speak to the king. "It's true, your grace. We were out flying for enjoyment and were attacked by terror birds. We came close to Gristnak while traveling around the storm."

Bogden stood. "Let's take this conversation to a more comfortable setting. I'm sure you both are tired."

TWENTY

T HEY FOLLOWED THE KING to a living room with a large fireplace. On the way, they had passed by a window that was being pounded by rain, but here, deeper in the stronghold, Kade wouldn't know there was a storm outside. There were bookcases on either side of the fireplace, as well as trinkets and paintings. A table at the other end of the room was covered with scrolls and books, a few sitting open.

Kade didn't know what he'd thought Gristnak would be like. Maybe dark, primitive, smelly. Not so civilized and clean. The air inside was fresh, and the goblins didn't live much differently from the dwarves.

Bogden's wife, Queen Sosie, brought in tea and two trays of food. She set them on a coffee table between two sofas. Sosie had silver hair that was in a shoulder-length braid, and her skin was light green. One eye was blue and one was green. She wore a light purple dress with a golden sash around her waist. Sosie was pretty for a goblin.

Kade and Griffin sat on one sofa, and the king and queen settled down on the other one. Bogden set his crown on an end table.

"I'm so sorry about your captain," Sosie said sympathetically. "We'll offer whatever help you need with his remains, as well as his dragon's."

"Thank you, your grace," Griffin said. She pulled her gloves off and poured herself a cup of tea. Kade shook his head when she offered him some. That earned him another displeased look from her.

The setting was comfortable. The room was warm. The sofa cushions were soft. The food and tea looked appetizing. Despite all that, Kade couldn't relax.

Peace had been reached with Gristnak over the last sixty years because of the work of Bogden and his father, Oren. Distrust between the races had caused the process to be slow. These goblins and the dwarves now focused on trading with each other instead of fighting over riches and resources. A celebration would be held after Griffin's wedding to officially acknowledge the alliance of five dwarf kingdoms with Gristnak, with pomp and circumstance.

"I think the last time I saw you was when you were barely a teenager, Princess," Bogden said. "How is your brother? I heard he got married a few months ago."

"Skylar is doing well. He and Zaina are very happy together. They'll be home soon from their trip."

"I'm glad to hear that," Sosie said. She looked at Bogden lovingly. "Finding your soulmate is one of the greatest pleasures this world can offer you."

The goblin king picked up one of his wife's hands and kissed the back of it. "Indeed, it is."

Kade could at least agree with that.

"The terror bird riders surprised us," Griffin said. "I wasn't aware that you had them."

Bogden grinned. "They were supposed to be revealed during the celebration. We surprised ourselves with how well it went to raise terror birds in captivity and train them to bear riders. But I suppose hatching dragons in captivity for the first time had its risks. Is that right, Kade?"

Griffin gave him a pointed look over her teacup that he read as, "Answer, and be nice."

Kade nodded. "The two brothers put all their faith in the gods and themselves that it would work."

"Goblins put little stock in gods," Bogden said. "We are molded from rock and stone, and to that, we return. We have faith in ourselves and our own strength. And the terror birds have been a game changer for patrolling the kingdom and monitoring activity in Raggerath. You have to have an extra advantage when your neighbor is constantly trying to kill you. Now, I don't know about keeping dragons, except maybe one of the miniature ones."

Griffin's eyes lit up. "There are miniature dragons?"

Bogden nodded. "You didn't know?"

"No, but I'd sure like to."

Kade hadn't heard of this either.

Bogden turned to Sosie. "Sweetie, you know more about them than I do."

"Yes. A cousin told me. The dragons are tiny enough to hold in your arms. There are few in captivity. Dwarves keep them on the coast somewhere. I think in Seareene."

Griffin couldn't be a dragon rider, but that wouldn't stop her from owning a small one. Seareene was far away to the northeast in Vuustwern, though. It would take days to travel there, even on dragonback. Too far to go pick up a new pet. But judging from her wide grin and sparkling eyes, she'd find a way.

"Back to the matter of Nafrag," Bogden said, "would you plan to strike against him now that he's killed a dragon rider?"

Griffin looked at Kade, and he shook his head. No action would be taken unless the goblins attacked Drangrere directly in force. Magus would blame Alden for flying too close to Raggerath.

"I don't think my father will see a counterstrike as necessary at this time," Griffin said with a frown.

"Even with the dragons, we can't wipe them out unless they're in the open," Kade added.

Bogden furrowed his brow. "That's unfortunate. I was about to send word to Amos in Carodhall and Magus that Nafrag appears to be massing troops both from within Raggerath and from outside groups of goblins, but for what purpose, we don't know. My terror bird riders can't get near because of the ballistae, and that activity is probably what drew Alden in. You'll need to keep a careful eye on your borders."

The next few minutes were spent in silence, besides the crackling of the fireplace. Kade had settled down enough to sit more relaxed but not to enjoy the refreshments.

Griffin spoke, "Lord Bogden, have you or your people seen a creature that's as large as a troll, covered in hair, and has horns on its head?"

He nodded. "Yes. Well, not the horns, but two weeks ago, Riggs saw something on the northern border at the edge of the Dragon's Tail that he thought was a troll, but he swore it was covered in hair. It didn't have horns, so maybe it was a female. That's what my research project over there is." He pointed at the other table. "I'm scouring history books and bestiaries to find any account of a creature that looks like that, but I haven't had any luck yet. I'll keep an eye out for mentions of horns."

"My husband will talk your ears off with stories from his research," Sosie said with a smile.

"I actually read a fascinating tale about how terror birds got their name. They were originally known as—"

There was a knock on the door.

"Come in," Bogden said.

It was Emery. "The storm has passed. I'll be leaving immediately to guard the bodies." Kade didn't feel confident about Emery's stony expression. That goblin prince better keep Alden and Onyx safe.

Griffin stood. "We also need to get going before my parents send out a search party. Your graces, it was wonderful to visit with you both. It will be a pleasure if you attend my wedding."

"We will be honored to come," Bogden said.

Sosie hugged Griffin. "At the wedding, I would like you to meet my daughter, Calista. She's close to your age, and she'll be queen one day. But she's nervous about it. Maybe you could give her some advice."

"I'd love to speak with her."

Bogden shook Kade's hand. "I am sorry for your loss. I hope one day, you'll get vengeance for Alden and Onyx."

Kade nodded. "I hope so, too."

Sosie came to hug him, but he flinched away.

"Oh, I'm sorry," she said.

Kade scrambled to think of what to say. "I apologize, my lady. I've had conflicts with goblins several times." Including what just happened to two of his team members. He paused awkwardly.

Sosie nodded. "I understand. Not all of our people like dwarves. There's still animosity. It may take generations for that to change."

"We'll walk you out," Bogden said. "I want to see the dragon."

They made their way to the entrance. Emerald was sleeping peacefully. A crowd of onlookers had gathered, but the goblins kept their distance, some peeking out from behind the columns.

The sky had cleared, and the stone in the courtyard was wet. Emerald opened her eyes and sat up as Kade approached. She rumbled in greeting, and he rubbed her head.

Bogden and Sosie stayed back and watched.

"Isn't she beautiful?" Griffin said.

They stared with wide eyes but didn't come closer.

The queen grinned. "She's magnificent."

"I think I prefer the terror birds," Bogden said. "They're smaller, at least. But I also read about a legend that if a brave dwarf, who is pure at heart, is killed by dragon fire, they will be reincarnated as a dragon. Although, whoever told that story forgot to say if goblins are included." Bogden waved a hand. "Anyway, I'll be sending word to your father soon, Princess. You two have a safe flight."

"Goodbye. I'll see you at the wedding."

Finally, they were leaving. Climbing up from the floor was the most difficult way to mount an adult dragon of Emerald's size, and he made sure that Griffin did okay. Falling in front of the goblins would be embarrassing.

Then a heaviness descended on him. How would he tell his team that Alden and Onyx were dead? Bogden and Sosie waved as Emerald took flight through the hole in the mountain.

TWENTY-ONE

T HEY ARRIVED HOME RIGHT before sunset. Emerald flew through the eyrie entrance and landed clumsily. She was probably tired.

Shona came to Emerald's side as they dismounted. "Where've you been? The king keeps asking when you're going to be home. And we had a situation. While they were on patrol, Jaheem and Barret had to chase away a dragon that was attacking a caravan. Apparently, it wasn't that big, but Barret had Smoky pursue it far into the wilderness while the beast wailed the whole time."

"I had to make sure it wouldn't come back," Barret said.

Shona threw an annoyed look at him. "The noise Jaheem said it was making could have attracted a larger dragon."

"We know all about that," Griffin mumbled.

"Smoky could've outrun it," Barret said confidently. "He's faster than any dragon."

Kade's head hurt as his team members bickered. He dismounted and helped Griffin down. Then he removed his headgear and opened and closed his mouth, swallowing hard. It felt as if someone had stabbed him in the gut with a knife.

"Kade, what's wrong?" Shona asked.

"Alden should never have ventured into goblin lands by himself, and now he's dead," Magus said and leaned his head against one hand.

The team had gathered in the great hall to tell the king the bad news. The other riders had taken it about as badly as Kade expected. They hadn't wanted to believe him. Shona's eyes were red from crying.

The king sighed and rubbed his hands together. "You said the bodies are in Gristnak?"

"Yes, sir," Kade said. "Bogden sent goblin warriors and terror bird riders to stand guard. Onyx's body can't be transported, and Alden would want to stay with her." The team had agreed on this earlier. "I'll explain to his family what happened. Onyx will have a cairn, and Alden will be burned, as is the tradition of the dragon riders." Kade took a breath as he held back tears.

Magus raised his eyebrows. "You said terror bird riders?"

"Yes, your grace."

"Anyway, that plan is fine with me," Magus said. "I'll send word to Bogden in the morning. I assume all of you will travel to Gristnak?"

Kade nodded.

"There's one more thing. Before he departed, Alden told me that should anything happen to him,

Kade would replace him as captain. That was his last wish, and I intend to respect it."

Kade felt weak at his knees. Griffin smiled at him, but he couldn't share the sentiment. He was only supposed to be the captain temporarily. The king stared at him expectantly.

"Your grace, I will be honored to accept the position." No matter how much doubt swirled inside, he needed to respect Alden's wish, too.

"Then it's official. So, Captain, when you are ready, you may take your team to Gristnak to pay respects to your fallen comrades. That will be all."

Kade looked at the team, his team now, as the king left.

Jaheem patted him on the back. "Congratulations."

"You'll do great," Shona said. "And we're all here for you."

Barret looked shocked and disappointed. Then he huffed and stomped away.

Kenji squeezed Kade's shoulder. "He'll get over it."

Griffin bounded up and hugged him. "I'm so happy for you. I don't know what Barret's problem is. Let me know if he causes you trouble."

Kade grimaced, and his stomach roiled. "I can handle him. I just want to focus on getting through the funeral first."

TWENTY-TWO

T HE TEAM FLEW TO Gristnak two days later in the afternoon. Bogden was waiting at the site with a group of goblins. Warriors were posted around the bodies. Sosie and Emery were there, as well as a young female goblin with silver shoulder-length hair and one blue eye and one green eye. That must be Calista.

They all wore black. Emery shifted from one foot to the other and looked bored. Two terror bird riders stood a little distance away. Riggs was one of them.

Jade growled at the terror birds. "Hush, boy," Kenji said. "It's all right."

Kade gave his team time to pay their respects to Alden and Onyx. The goblins had maneuvered the dragon onto her belly in a position that made her look as though she was sleeping. Her saddle had been removed and set neatly off to the side. Alden's armor had been tied to the saddle. One of the dragons would carry the gear back to the eyrie.

The double-headed axe lay on top of the saddle because the head had broken off the haft. A light layer of blood still stained the rocks, but the rain had washed most of it away.

Alden lay on a pyre. The crossbow bolts had been removed, and the single-headed axe from his saddle lay on his chest, his hands gripping the haft.

Jaheem wrapped an arm around Shona as she started crying again. Kenji kneeled next to Onyx and stroked her head. He pressed a hand against his eyes, and his shoulders shook.

Barret stood next to Alden. His chin trembled, and he bowed his head. The dragons each approached Onyx, sniffed her, and made distressed noises.

When the team was ready to proceed, they took Alden's axe, and then two male goblins in black garb wrapped the rider's body in dark blue cloth. Kade pulled out his knife and removed a scale from Onyx's side. It would be put in a shadow box and hung on the wall alongside the others in the war room.

He wrapped it in a cloth and stowed it safely away in one of Emerald's saddlebags, along with the broken axe. Alden's body was ready, but first, each of them found a rock and placed them next to Onyx.

"We'll finish the cairn for you," Bogden said when they walked back.

"Thank you," Kade replied.

They lined up on one side of the pyre.

Jaheem nudged him. "You can do the honors."

Kade sniffled and swallowed hard. "Emerald." The dragon came to stand at Alden's head. He pointed to the pyre. "Fire."

She breathed flames onto Alden's body, and Kade let some tears fall. As the fire burned, he prayed to the gods that if an afterlife existed, Alden would be reunited with Ada, and maybe Onyx, too.

He didn't know how long they stood there watching. Kade was barely aware of when it was time to go home. His heart felt heavy, and his head was in a fog. They said goodbye to Bogden and his family and mounted their dragons. Goblins were working on the cairn. Shona directed Topaz to pick up Onyx's saddle.

The dragons seemed to be grieving because they flew home with little gusto. Kade wasn't excited to go back to Drangrere. His life would never be the same, and he wasn't ready for it.

TWENTY-THREE

G RIFFIN STARED AT THE two black candles she had
lit. They sat on the coffee table in front of
her and were covered so her cat wouldn't set his
fur on fire. Sir Whiskers lounged on her lap. She
stroked his soft fur and leaned back against the sofa.
It was quiet in the living room, so she could mourn
in peace.

The riders should be home soon. They couldn't
stay away too long and ignore their duties, despite
the circumstances. Griffin hoped no calls for help
would come in today. The team deserved time to
grieve.

She closed her eyes and leaned her head
back. She wouldn't trade her experience of flying
yesterday for the world, but what if it had been her,
Kade, and Emerald lying dead in that valley? For the
first time, Griffin understood that being a dragon
rider wasn't something to be taken lightly. It was
fun, but it was perilous. This was why royals didn't
become dragon riders.

She heard the door open, and Kade walked into
the room. The devastated expression on his face
had her setting Sir Whiskers on the sofa and going
to hug him.

"I lit candles for them," she said.

Kade pulled away and nodded. "The funeral went well. We'll go back soon to see the cairn."

Griffin held his face in her hands. "Are you okay? Or is that a pointless question?"

Kade took hold of her hands and held them. His expression was pinched, and his eyes were downcast. When he looked up, the weight of the world seemed to fill his eyes.

"I don't know if I can be the captain."

"Don't doubt yourself, Kade. Yesterday, when everything was trying to kill us, you were cool, calm, and collected while I was freaking out, and you kept us both safe. Alden chose you for a reason, and I believe he made the right decision. I'm sure anyone would feel nervous about taking this post." Kade opened his mouth, but she beat him to it. "Except Barret."

He rubbed the back of his neck and shook his head. "Why didn't he choose Barret? He was next in line, and he's capable of being the captain."

Griffin shrugged. "You can argue with Alden when it's your turn to join him, which I hope won't be for a long time. Do you think Cobalt and Sandstone know yet that their mother is never coming home?"

"I showed them the scale that I took off Onyx. Then they plopped in their nest and had mournful looks on their faces, so I think they understood."

"Poor babies." They didn't deserve to lose their mother like that.

"I'm sure Crystal knows what happened, too."

"Do you want to come sit and have a cup of tea?"

He shook his head. "I have to go back to the eyrie. And I don't think Sir Whiskers will welcome my company. I feel safer around the dragons than I do with him."

Griffin looked at her cat, who was giving Kade a hard stare. Silly kitty.

"I guess you're right. Let me know if you need anything. I'm here for you."

Kade gave a little smile. "Thank you."

He left, and Griffin sat with her cat again. She stroked his head. "I worry about him. I almost wish I wasn't getting married because he needs me more than Erik right now." A pang of sadness hit her. After she moved to Carodhall, she didn't know if or when she would see Kade again.

"I'll just have to be there for him while I can and pray to the gods to help make him the best captain possible."

Sir Whiskers purred contentedly while Griffin fretted.

TWENTY-FOUR

T HE FIRST FEW DAYS weren't so bad, considering he had already been acting captain. Kade had let the team know that he had spotted Syrene and that they needed to keep an eye out for her and Zallar on the southern border. And they needed to watch for goblin troops from Raggerath to the south and the west.

He had also gone to find Alden's brother, but Jacob and his family had moved. A friend of theirs promised to send a message to them after she found out what settlement they were living in now.

The team was still numb from Ada's death, and everyone dealt with the loss of Alden and Onyx the best they could. The somber silence that overtook the eyrie was eventually replaced with resolve to honor the fallen rider by protecting and defending the kingdom just as fiercely and passionately as he had.

Barret continued with his brooding. The other rider followed orders because he had to, but he walked around with a tense posture and eyes full of anger. Kenji observed in pensive silence, Jaheem reassured Kade that things would improve, and

Shona worried that Barret would leave the team. They couldn't go on like this indefinitely.

Kade didn't know what to say to make peace, so he continued to send the other rider away to get the metaphorical storm clouds that followed him around out of the eyrie. "Barret, go on patrol. Barret, bring the broken axe to the blacksmiths to be repaired. Barret, bring a message to this place or to that place."

And he made it a point not to patrol with him for now. "Barret, I'm taking Shona on patrol. Stay here."

"Shona had Topaz out this morning. Smoky's fresher," he said.

"It was a short flight," Shona said. "You know how much he loves flying. Topaz will be okay."

"Smoky will be faster if you need to come find us," Kade said. He didn't turn around to see how Barret reacted.

He made plans with Maysie and looked forward to getting out of the eyrie for a while again.

"Ow, Sapphire."

Kade adjusted the hatchling in his arms. She had stuck a foot underneath his coat and grabbed his tunic. Her talons poked through to his skin. Sapphire occasionally squirmed and let out excited squeaks at seeing so many dwarves, as well as anything shiny that caught her eye. The hatchling had a sweet temperament, always loving to meet new people. She scratched at the neck collar of the miniature saddle strapped to her back.

"Stop that." Kade grabbed her foot before she got a toe hung. "I know you don't like it, but you have to get used to it."

Kade exited the stronghold and followed a path to the right that led to the overlook. Maysie waited for him there. She wore a beautiful green dress with a flower pattern and a green coat.

Kade ended up always wearing his blue coat, blue long-sleeved tunic, and the blue-and-silver pants that were his uniform. He had a white long-sleeved shirt on, but it wasn't visible. Kade remembered to wear a nicer pair of boots.

Maysie smiled and tilted her head when she saw Sapphire. "Who is this?"

"I thought you seemed nervous about meeting Emerald, so, on Shona's advice, I brought Sapphire so you can start with a smaller dragon."

He set the hatchling down on the parapet that ran along the edge of the overlook. Sapphire stared at Maysie for a moment and then went up to her with a friendly rumble.

"Hi, little one." Maysie hesitantly reached her hand out. She snapped it back when Sapphire moved her head closer and nervously laughed. "Do they bite?"

"No. She won't hurt you. You can pet her neck or her chest if you don't want to touch her head. Dragons raised in captivity are docile and friendly. And while they're young, we work hard to socialize them with other dwarves. She won't do anything except smell you."

Maysie reached out again and stroked Sapphire's neck. The hatchling purred happily. "I was confused when you told me not to wear a lot of jewelry."

"They like shiny things." It was important to him for Maysie not to be scared. If he married her, dragons would always be a part of their lives.

"What's the deal with the little saddle?"

"It's so they get used to wearing them. It's easier to start training them while they're small." Sapphire looked at the sky. It was mostly clear, but clouds were rolling in from the north. "You want to fly? Go on. Go fly."

Sapphire leaped off the parapet and circled above them higher and higher.

"Will she fly away?" Maysie asked worriedly.

"No. She knows who feeds her. We just have to watch that she's not attacked by a hawk or an eagle. Years ago, though, a wild dragon named Carnelian was hatched in the eyrie, and he didn't settle in. He hardly cooperated with training and destroyed a few miniature saddles. There was too much wild in him."

"What happened to him?"

"Before a rider could be found, he left the eyrie and never came back. There were too many male dragons on the team at the time so that may've played a role. We assume he flew into the wild and found a mate."

Kade leaned against the parapet, and Maysie stood next to it. They looked out over the landscape. Kade breathed a sigh of relief. Spending time with Maysie was peaceful compared to what he was dealing with in the eyrie. She was sweet and made good company, and he could relax.

"Were you scared when you first met a dragon?" she asked curiously.

Kade only caught the last couple of words. "I'm sorry. I was distracted. What did you say?"

"Were you scared when you first met a dragon?"

"A bit. When I was a child, I snuck into the eyrie at night. Emerald was the first dragon I met."

Maysie raised her eyebrows. "That was either brave or stupid."

"I knew the dragons wouldn't hurt me. Alden caught me, and he encouraged me to wait for an opening on the team when I was older. And not to sneak into the eyrie again." Alden had played such an important part in his life. "I really miss him."

Maysie grabbed one of his hands and squeezed it comfortingly. "I'm sorry you lost him."

Kade nodded. "Thank you." He noticed that Maysie wore a red rose pin on her coat. The colored parts looked like gemstones, and they were bordered with silver. "That pin is pretty."

"Thank you. I made it. Every year, if we can, my mom and I go to a spring festival in Finsteria," she said. "They're well known for their numerous rose varieties, although I love classic red roses. One time when I was little, I wandered away into a wooded area. Some gnarled and twisted old trees surrounded a tiny glade that was full of wildflowers. It seemed magical and brought stories of fairies to my mind. There was a hole, like a burrow, dug out in the center, and when I looked inside, an animal stared back at me. I don't know if it's fright that made my memory foggy, but I swear there were more than two tiny eyes."

"What happened next?"

"I stared at it. It stared at me. And I sprinted back to my mom and have avoided that glade ever since. You fly out to so many places. Have you seen anything like that?"

Kade shook his head. "Don't worry. If I'm with you, I won't let a monster in a hole hurt you."

"My hero." She gazed at him lovingly and gave him a side hug. "So, you're the captain of the dragon riders now. That means you'll be even busier?" She scratched at a fingernail.

"I have to organize patrols and go on calls and keep a close eye on our stock of food, weapons, and other materials. I spoke with the leathersmiths and the saddlers about building more saddles. And I had to make plans for when the adult dragons will gorge next. It can be exhausting, but I can still make time for us."

Maysie tilted her head. "Gorge?"

"We feed the adults a couple of sheep, pigs, or goats twice a week, but at least twice a month, hunters bring us large game like ibexes, mountain goats, antelopes, and boars. The bodies are put in an area below the eyrie, and the dragons can eat as much as they want."

"Oh." She wrinkled her nose.

The gorging wasn't a pretty sight, but the dragons had to eat. A comfortable silence passed between him and Maysie for a few minutes.

"I like this," she said. "Us. You're the most honorable man I've ever met. I feel safe with you."

Warmth spread through his chest, and he shifted closer so that their bodies touched. "I like us being together, too. I've always placed all my energy and focus on the dragons. I never thought I'd find someone as important to me as they are."

Maysie put her hand against his cheek, and his heart beat faster. They went in for a kiss, but then two loud male voices interrupted them. It was two older dwarves arguing about whether tomatoes were considered fruits or vegetables.

Kade watched Sapphire, and Maysie looked at the landscape. The dwarves finally passed by, but so had the moment.

"I have to go," Maysie said. "It was nice to meet Sapphire."

Kade kissed Maysie on the cheek. "I'll come and see you soon."

That earned him a loving smile again. "I'll hold you to that."

He gazed at her as she followed the path back to the stronghold. Kade stayed outside for a little while longer, his body feeling lighter and his head clearer. Then he whistled for Sapphire. The hatchling dived toward him and landed on the parapet. He unsaddled her and picked her up.

"Kade!" Shona called. She ran up to him, breathing hard and with worry in her eyes.

"What's wrong?"

"We just got word that trolls are attacking Dally Springs."

TWENTY-FIVE

K ADE AND SHONA HURRIED to the eyrie. She carried Sapphire to the nursery so he could go to his quarters and armor up. Trolls attacking a settlement in the middle of the day? This rarely happened. When he went into the eyrie, Emerald was saddled.

Crystal had sat up in her nest and watched them with interest. When they flew out, she stood as if she was going to follow. Kade looked over his shoulder as they left, but Crystal stayed in the eyrie. That was for the best. He didn't want a rogue dragon flying around with no rider controlling it.

Dally Springs was not too far to the north. It was an older settlement on the western edge of the kingdom that had seldom seen trouble. The springs were in a narrow canyon, and the walls of the Blood Spear Mountains provided natural protection.

As they neared the settlement, Kade sat up and indicated to Jaheem, Shona, and Kenji to go on the attack. He held a hand out to Barret to stay behind on overwatch. With the increasing cloud cover, Smoky would be camouflaged in the sky.

There were three large trolls. A fourth one had been killed by a ballista bolt.

As captain, Kade got first dibs on attacking. Two of the trolls had breached the stone wall. It was crumbling in places and in sore need of repair. One ballista on the wall had been destroyed, and the other two sat at bad angles.

As expected, the trolls were being mindful to avoid them. Some buildings had been damaged, but because most were stone, they were faring better. One fire burned but was unlikely to spread.

Kade pulled his spear out and leaned forward. This should be a routine job. "Attack, Emerald."

The dragon stooped and chose her target. The troll was bloody from several wounds and had a spear in its shoulder. Distracted by the soldiers, it never saw Emerald coming. She landed hard on it, and the wooden club flew out of its hand and rolled into the middle of the street.

The head of the club had sharp stones driven into it to make spikes. Blood sprayed as Emerald went in for the kill. A blue shape zoomed overhead. Topaz attacked another troll that was wielding a stone spear.

Emerald raised her head and licked blood from her jaws. The last troll ran back through the wall. Kade looked up to see Jade stooping on it. But then he saw a flash of gray. Smoky was also stooping. What was Barret doing?

Kade gasped when Smoky and Jade collided, the gray dragon too fast to stop his momentum, and the green dragon too focused on his target. The earth shook as both dragons crashed to the ground, their talons grasping at stone and rocks to avoid rolling onto their riders.

Jade was twice the age of Smoky and larger. They were both big enough to hurt each other. Jade let out a deep, angry roar at Smoky. It was fortunate that their nests were on opposite ends of their row.

The gray dragon squealed as he slipped into the springs, splashing a huge wave of water onto the rocks. The springs were warm but not dangerously so. Heat didn't bother dragons.

Kade let go of the breath he was holding. Both dragons and their riders looked unharmed. Hot anger spread through his body. Barret was a dead man. The troll turned around, raised its stolen dwarf spear, and charged toward the grounded dragons.

"Emerald, go."

She took flight and flew over Smoky and Jade, but the troll dived out of the way. Emerald slipped on the wet rocks and went down. She let out a frustrated roar. Kade held on as he was thrown around, and the harness dug in painfully.

A line of fire lit up the ground in front of him, and he closed his eyes and held his arm over his face as hot air buffeted him, stealing his breath away. When Kade could look again, he saw Topaz trying to keep the troll at bay, but they were farther in the canyon where the dragon couldn't turn in the narrow space to attack.

Before the brute chose its next target, Ruby pounced on it. The fight was over. Kade glared under his scarf at Barret. The other rider turned his head toward him for a moment. Kade couldn't see his face, but Barret leaned against the pommel of the saddle with his head in his hands. The rest of the team gathered.

Kade didn't care what had attracted the trolls to the settlement. He wouldn't have lost any sleep if the last one escaped. All he was focused on right now was what he was going to do with Barret when they got back to the eyrie.

Twenty-Six

I T TOOK LONGER THAN he would have liked to speak with the baron, but Cyril must've noticed the fuming expression on Kade's face. Also, he couldn't keep still because his sides and his legs hurt from where he'd been thrown around in the harness.

Cyril let them go, saying that he would send a report to the king. Jaheem informed Kade that Smoky and Jade weren't injured besides a few lost scales. Emerald wasn't hurt either. Kade didn't want to look at Barret as they flew to the eyrie.

After they landed, his hands shook so much that he struggled to unclip himself. He dismounted and ripped his harness and his headgear off. The helmet clanged loudly when he threw it to the floor. Kade couldn't hold his anger in anymore. He stomped across the room to Barret.

"What was that?" he shouted.

Barret flinched, and then he glared and stood tall. "You held me back on purpose! Lately, you keep sending me away, and you won't fly with me unless you have no other choice!"

"You want to know why I haven't wanted to be around you? It's because you've been so hostile ever since Alden made me the captain! I know you wanted the position, but it wasn't my fault that you got stepped over! So, stop acting like an adversary and start being a team member again!" Kade took a breath. A weight seemed to lift off his chest at voicing what he had held in for weeks.

Smoky growled and had a warning in his gray eyes. Barret rubbed the dragon's chin. The other riders stood silently in shock.

"As far as the mission," Kade continued, "I had you stay on overwatch because Smoky blended with the clouds, and he could dive the quickest if we needed him. Otherwise, I may've sent you on the attack."

Barret looked at his boots with shame in his eyes.

Yes, idiot, there was a plan, not a vendetta. As the anger drained from his body, exhaustion weighed him down. "You're cleaning all the saddles and any of the weapons that need it." Kade put as much firmness in his voice as he could. "You're lucky I'm not kicking you off the team. You or Kenji or one of the dragons could've been killed, and we've had too much loss lately."

Barret snapped his head up, his eyes wide and filled with guilt.

Kade had nothing else to say. He turned on his heel and went to unsaddle Emerald. Then he left the eyrie.

Kade sat on his bed in his quarters, decompressing. He was used to Alden scolding them or occasionally dishing out a punishment, but now that was his role. Being the captain wasn't easy. Maybe it wasn't supposed to be. Kade would much rather be hanging out with Maysie than having to deal with this.

He tapped his fingers on the bed. The quarters for the dragon riders each had a fireplace and were furnished with the bare necessities. Otherwise, the riders were free to add anything they wanted. Kade had mostly kept his the same.

There was a bed, a chest, a table with two chairs, a mirror on the wall, a dresser, a desk with a chair, and a stand for his armor and weapons. A previous rider had left a leather armchair and an ottoman. There had been a bookshelf, but he had given it to Shona. Except for a few personal possessions, he only needed what was necessary.

The dragons were his life, which was why his wooden dragon toy from his childhood and the carved dragon's tooth that Griffin had given him a few years ago as a birthday present were his favorite items. Both sat on top of the dresser along with the box full of damaged coins that he had found in the wild.

Kade headed back to the eyrie to check on the eggs. Barret sat on a stool and dutifully wiped his saddle with a cloth while Smoky slept with his head near his rider. Crystal was up. She nudged Barret's back.

He stopped wiping and turned around. "Crystal, cut it out."

"What's wrong?" Kade asked.

Barret startled and looked at him with an uncertain gaze. Then he got back to cleaning. "I don't know. She keeps bothering me."

"Crystal, girl," Kade walked up to her, "what's going on?"

The dragon bumped his chest with her nose, and he petted her. Kade then picked up her saddle.

"Do you want to go riding? Is that it?"

Crystal sniffed the saddle. Then she lay back down. She didn't lower herself into the saddling position, so Kade returned the saddle to the rack. He grabbed another stool and sat next to her. Crystal lay her head on the floor and nudged his legs for attention. She purred as he petted her.

"I'll keep her busy for you," Kade said.

"Thanks." Barret put his saddle on Smoky's rack. Then he went and picked up Jade's. The dragon cracked open a green eye and let out a low growl. "I know. You hate me right now."

Kade kept stroking Crystal while Barret used a brush on the saddle first. An awkward silence stretched between the two riders.

"You were right," Barret said. "I was angry when Alden chose you to be the captain, but I wasn't entirely mad at you. Typically, the succession of leadership goes to the most senior member, and I had it built up in my mind that I was next in line to be captain. When Alden didn't choose me, I thought he didn't believe I could do it. I've worked hard since I joined the dragon riders, and I felt like I deserved the position. And after he died, I couldn't ask him why I wasn't chosen. My ego and jealousy got the best of me. I have been an ass lately, and I understand why you didn't want to be around me. I'm sorry for that and for acting stupid on the mission."

The stormy tension dissipated. "No one got hurt," Kade said. "It's okay. Just don't do it again."

"You know, you've got guts confronting me like that in front of Smoky. He could've eaten you. What did Alden always say? Never start trouble in the eyrie, or the dragons will finish it. I didn't think you had that in you." Barret looked him in the eyes. "Kade, I'm your team member, and I'm your friend. If Alden felt that you're the best choice to be the captain, then I need to respect that, not pull ridiculous stunts to prove my worth. You've kept the team running strong ever since he left."

Relief settled over Kade. "Thank you. And just because Alden hadn't picked you doesn't mean he didn't believe in you. He told me that you have potential. And I agree that you would be a great captain one day, too. That's why I've decided that if we can build another eyrie, I want you to command that team."

Barret's eyebrows shot up. "Even after all the chaos that I caused today?"

Kade nodded. "You've always deserved the chance to lead a team."

Barret smiled. "That means a lot to hear you say that. Why didn't you kick me off the team? I almost think Alden would have."

"Because you're my friend, and I wanted to believe that you'd respect me one day as the captain."

"I respect you, Kade."

"Thanks." This was how things should have always been between them. Crystal was asleep, so Kade stood. "Apologize to Kenji, and offer Jade a nice fat pig as a peace offering."

"Yes, sir."

Kade went into the nursery. Cobalt, Sandstone, and Sapphire were napping in their nest. He checked on the eggs. They were still warm. As he turned away, the orange egg looked as if it moved, but he wasn't sure. Kade watched for a moment, but nothing else happened. He shrugged and left.

TWENTY-SEVEN

K ADE AND BARRET WALKED into the council room, where the king held meetings. All the captains of the different units of the army were there and casually spoke with each other. This meeting was held about twice a month. Light streamed in from windows to the right. A long wooden table sat in the center of the room with a candle chandelier hanging above it.

Kade straightened his coat out again. His stomach was doing flips, and he kept wiping away sweat from his hands. Barret had come with him this time to provide moral support, which Kade was grateful for.

A red-haired dwarf woman approached them. She was Breanna, captain of the archers, and currently, the only woman of her rank. "Congratulations on your promotion, Kade."

"Thank you, ma'am."

"Alden was a good man and a good leader. You have big shoes to fill."

Thanks. Walking past an empty dragon nest and staring at Alden's equipment and weapons every day was enough of a reminder. Kade nodded and smiled, though. "I hope to make him proud."

The others came to congratulate him, and judging from their scrutinizing looks, to size him up. Eventually, the king arrived. Everyone bowed and found seats. Kade sat at the far end of the table with Barret on his right and Thayer, the captain of the cavalry, on his left.

The other dwarf had a bushy beard and long blond hair that was partly braided back. Kade picked up the smell of hay and ponies from the dwarf, but he couldn't judge. He had heard many times that the scent of dragon clung to the riders, despite them not being aware of it.

"Let's begin," Magus said. "We'll start on my left this time."

One by one, the captains gave their reports on how their units were doing. Kade had practiced what he was going to say several times. He bounced his leg and kept messing with his hands.

Barret put a hand on his shoulder. "Calm down," he whispered.

Harrison, captain of the men-at-arms, was staring at Kade with a quirked eyebrow from across the table. He had blue eyes, short black hair, and a short beard. Luckily, the dwarf was then distracted with giving his report. Kade sat up straight and folded his hands together. He ran through his own report in his head one more time and looked at the table. In front of him and Barret were deep scratches that didn't seem natural. They were long and thin and went against the grain of the wood.

Kade ran his fingers over them and caught Barret's eye. The other rider nodded and felt the scratches, too. Flynn and Lucas had once taken the young Sapphire and Moonstone to a captains' meeting, but the dragons hadn't been on their best behavior that day.

Harrison finished his report.

"Captain Kade?" Magus said.

His voice caught in his throat as everyone turned their heads toward him. Barret tapped him on the leg with his foot.

"Yes, your grace," Kade said. "The dragon riders are doing well. We visited Alden and Onyx's gravesite yesterday, and the goblins did an excellent job with the cairn. They also raised one over what remained of Alden's body. Crystal's doing better. We hope to find a new rider for her soon."

Magus nodded. "That's great to hear. Your team has been down a rider, and now two, for long enough."

"Our patrols have shown no unusual activity besides the sighting of a large number of trolls near Miknare, but they were on the other side of the Dragon's Tail on the eastern edge of the kingdom. I warned the baron, and we will keep watch on that area. Attacks have decreased lately, but we don't know for how long."

"And what of the hatchlings?" Magus asked. "Are we keeping all of them?"

"Yes. We have room for them." This didn't seem like the right time to argue for a new eyrie, at least not in front of the other captains.

"Excellent," the king said. "If there's nothing else, we can move on to Thayer."

"That's all, your grace."

The others finished their reports, and they all stood as Magus exited the room. Kade and Barret left and headed to the eyrie.

"You did good at the meeting," Barret said.

"Thank you." They were back to being friends and being relaxed in each other's company.

"You know, if we keep Sapphire, Cobalt, and Sandstone, we'll have to give the other two away. We only have room to build two more nests."

"We'll deal with that problem later. I'm still holding out hope for another eyrie."

Kade spotted Griffin down a hallway, speaking with two other girls. The stronghold wasn't busy this afternoon, so the crowds were sparse. As they neared the skywalk, there was almost no one. Kade was distracted with looking outside when Barret tapped him on the arm.

"What?"

"Look," he said with furrowed brows and his mouth partly open.

Griffin stood in the skywalk.

Kade scratched his head. "Did you see her run by us?"

"No. How does she do that? There's no access here besides through this hallway."

They both bowed their heads as they approached her.

"I'd like to hang out in the eyrie for a bit," she said.

Kade nodded. "That's fine. But first, how do you pull off beating us here? Because I spotted you way back there, and you never passed us. And this isn't the only time you've done it."

Griffin had a cat that ate the canary look on her face. "I'm the princess. I'm allowed to have my secrets."

"There must be tunnels and a hidden door," Barret said as he scanned the wall. "But I can't figure out where."

"Guys, guys, come quick!" Shona said. She was running toward them.

Kade feared that they had to go on another call, but she was grinning.

"The eggs are hatching."

TWENTY-EIGHT

G RIFFIN HURRIED WITH THE riders to the eyrie and rushed into the nursery. Jaheem and Kenji watched the eggs, and the hatchlings stared intently from where they were bunched together on the chest.

Jaheem turned to them. "I walked in here, and the eggs were rocking like crazy. We moved them farther apart so they don't knock into each other."

Both eggs had fallen onto their sides and rolled to and fro in their cradle. Griffin would finally witness dragons hatching, something that only the riders got to see. The team watched with excitement on their faces.

A flash of light enveloped the orange egg and then the white one. A hatchling breathes fire to break the egg. There were crackling noises. Cracks and splits spread through the eggs, and then two baby dragons burst from them. They shook off and spread their wings, looking around curiously at their new environment.

Tears welled up in Griffin's eyes. The hatchlings were so precious. They looked at the dwarves and wobbled to the edge of the cradle, both making little squeaks.

Kade stepped forward. "Hey, little ones. Welcome to the world."

He extended a hand, and they sniffed it. The white dragon shimmered with the same brilliance as Crystal, and its eyes were blue. The orange one looked golden when the light shone on its scales just right. Kade gently wrapped his hands around the white hatchling and lifted it. It squirmed for a few seconds and then relaxed. He checked the gender.

"This one's a boy. Are we still in agreement on Quartz?"

The other riders nodded. Quartz wriggled again and made little squeaks. Kade had to hold him tighter. Shona picked up the orange hatchling. "This one's a girl, so Amber will be her name. Do you want to hold her, Princess?"

"Yes, please." She took Amber from Shona and cradled her. The hatchling relaxed in her arms, unlike her brother, who kept squirming as the others passed him around. He was going to be a feisty one. She turned her attention back to Amber. "Who's a little cutie?"

The hatchling stared at her with inquisitive orange eyes and purred. She was so tiny that half of her body fit in one of Griffin's hands. She gently stroked the dragon. It was important to socialize the hatchlings with dwarves as soon as possible. Then they would see them as their friends.

She eventually got to hold Quartz. He was larger, and he must have worn himself out because he behaved for her. "Just wait until the day when you're big enough to kill a troll. But for now, all you need to worry about is sleeping, eating, and growing."

Kenji then took Quartz, and Kade held Amber. They introduced them to the older hatchlings, who had waited patiently. Then they carried them into the eyrie. Crystal stood in the middle of the room as if she knew her eggs had hatched. Topaz was sitting up in his nest.

"Hey, Crystal," Kade said. "We have two little ones to introduce you to."

Crystal came forward and nuzzled the hatchlings. She rumbled with delight, and her babies made cooing noises. Kade and Kenji carried them to Topaz, who sniffed them and purred deeply.

After a few minutes, Quartz yawned, and Amber lay her head against Kade's arm, blinking sleepily. They were carried back into the nursery. Griffin helped pick up egg fragments, which Barret and Shona threw outside. Quartz and Amber were placed in the cradle. They curled up with each other, and Sapphire climbed in and encircled them with her body.

"Jaheem, tell the butchers that we'll need fresh blood," Kade said.

"Sure." The rider left.

Dragons ate nothing except meat and anything having to do with meat. Quartz and Amber would stay in the safety of the nursery for a few weeks before being let outside. Griffin gazed at them as they slept. They looked so fragile and vulnerable, but one day, they would be large, fire-breathing beasts.

"Come on, Griffin," Kade said. "Let them sleep."

"Thank you for letting me watch them hatch." She followed him out. "Witnessing it was a pleasure and an honor that I'll never forget."

"By the way, I had sent a letter to the new captain of the dragon riders in Carodhall, Percy. I told him how great you are with dragons, and he agreed to let you spend time with their team whenever you want."

The sides of her mouth hurt from how much she was smiling. Griffin hugged Kade tightly. "Thank you. Thank you. You're the best friend ever." Then she remembered something. "Oh, you and Barret are good, right?"

Kade gave her a confused look. "What do you mean?"

Barret walked up to them. "What's going on? I heard my name."

"A soldier in the skywalk eavesdropped on a heated argument between you guys two days ago," Griffin said. "You left the door open. I heard about it from a royal guard. What happens in the eyrie doesn't always stay in the eyrie, boys."

"We're fine," Kade said, and then he looked at Barret.

The other rider nodded. "Yes, Princess. No problems between us. It's all water under the bridge."

She smiled. "Good. I was worried."

For this moment, life was great.

Twenty-Nine

T HE PEACE WITH THE decreased calls didn't last long. Besides a brief flurry of snow, winter was losing its grip on the land, and over the next week and a half, pleasant weather brought a spike of troll and goblin attacks on settlements, travelers, and caravans with it. The heat of summer couldn't come soon enough.

As usual, if the settlement was mostly wood, damage and casualties were higher than if it had more stone. Extra ballistae sometimes bought more time. The thicker wooden walls held twice, which pleased the king, but those were the only exceptions.

The team increased patrols, but it wasn't enough. Then another call came in that goblins were attacking Hoeckan. It was late in the evening when the riders flew out, but by the time they arrived, the battle was over. Almost every structure that had been rebuilt was destroyed again, and the survivors had fled.

"The king still insists that we have to hold that area," Kade said to Maysie.

"Mm-hmm."

He looked at her. Maysie seemed to only be half paying attention to him. She stared at the red rose he had given her, running her fingers over a leaf. A bush grew wild on a mountainside near the eyrie.

"I'm sorry. We can talk about something else," he said.

"It's all right."

Kade had taken Maysie to the top of one of the watchtowers, somewhere peaceful where they could be alone. Despite how busy he was, he tried to make time to see her. The sun had fallen, and stars glittered in the clear night sky. He glanced at the stairs every once in a while to see if yet another date would be interrupted.

It had happened two out of three times already. A goblin attack on a caravan interrupted dinner with a game of checkers. Trolls harassing a settlement cut short an evening visit to Maysie's favorite shop, which had a book section. Meeting up with her at night wasn't ideal, but he'd been too tired to do it any earlier.

"We were also asked to escort a caravan that was transporting gold, which is nerve-wracking now because of what happened to Ada, but luckily, it went okay. Gold is the most likely cargo to encounter trouble with, especially from dragons."

"But I thought they covered stuff like that. How do the dragons know?" she asked him curiously.

"I have no idea how they figure it out. Even our dragons know, but they mind us when we tell them to ignore gold or other shiny cargo."

A roar split the air, and a dragon flew by the watchtower. Maysie gasped and backed away.

"It's okay. It's Topaz. He loves flying. He'd fly through thunderstorms and blizzards if we asked him to."

"Why don't we sit?" Maysie said, looking a little on edge.

"Sure."

The only place was on the floor. Maysie pulled her purple cloak around her and leaned against him. Kade wrapped an arm around her.

"You're more brooding than last time," she said as she laid the rose on her lap.

"It's frustrating when you command a power greater than thousands of soldiers, and you can't keep the kingdom safe. Alden tried so hard, and he entrusted me to continue his work. I feel like I'm failing him." Kade's chest ached. "The only good thing that's happened lately is that Amber and Quartz hatched and are healthy."

"If it's too stressful, why not find a different job?" Maysie asked.

Kade raised his eyebrows. "I'm a dragon rider. I have a duty."

"That duty can be somewhere else. My Uncle Harold was a stonemason, but he fell out of love with the job. So, he switched to being a cook. My Aunt Rosie was once determined to be a gardener, but she had a black thumb. Plants died soon after she put them into the ground or barely hung onto life. She put so much work into that pitiful garden, and then worms and snails overran it, devouring everything, even plants that are supposed to repel them. Aunt Rosie spent all day and night picking the pests off, but it was too late."

"What's the point of these stories?"

"That sometimes things aren't worth the trouble. Because of all the stress Aunt Rosie put herself through in that fruitless venture, she fell ill and never fully recovered. I appreciate everything you do as part of the dragon riders, but I don't want the job to tear you apart or for something horrible to happen to you, like with Alden. I care about you, Kade, and I love you."

Her words stunned him for a moment. He had feelings for her and could imagine her being his wife, but he hadn't known if she felt the same way about him. Kade looked through the windows across from him.

"While riding at night, I sometimes wonder if I can reach into the sky and pluck a star down. They're always too high up, though. But I don't need a star from the sky when I have one next to me."

Maysie cuddled closer. "You're more precious than any of the finest jewels I've ever seen."

She leaned in, and stars shone in her eyes. Kade cupped her face in his hands and kissed her. The world seemed to stand still. One moment of tranquility. One moment of peace. Then they pressed their foreheads together and grinned.

Kade breathed in easier as the ache in his chest disappeared. "Griffin's going-away party is next week. Do you want to be my date?"

Maysie gave him another quick kiss. "Yes. Why is she doing it so early?"

"She said it would be easier to handle."

"I guess that makes sense. Do you want to have supper with my parents this week?"

Kade pursed his lips. "I have to leave tomorrow. Jaheem, Kenji, and I are going to the Vuustwern border to escort Prince Skylar and Princess Zaina home. I'll be gone for three or four days."

She frowned and stood.

"Maysie?"

She pulled her cloak tighter around her. "I need to go to bed."

"I'm sorry."

She nodded. "I know." But she still looked despondent, and her shoulders were slumped.

"It's not too late. Do you want to come see the new hatchlings and Emerald?"

"Not right now. And I can find my way back if you want to stay here for a while. Thank you again for the rose. Good night."

Kade didn't feel like going back yet. Getting to sit was nice. "Good night. I love you." The words slipped out of his mouth easily.

She grinned. "I'll see you at the party or before then, if you have time."

Kade leaned against the wall and closed his eyes, enjoying a few more minutes of rest. But he couldn't stay for long. Back to the eyrie and whatever chaos that awaited. He also needed to reply to the latest letter his parents had sent. What would his life be like if he was a simple miner?

Kade banished the thought immediately. He didn't belong in the mines, trapped in the bowels of the earth in the darkness, the weight of the mountains bearing down on him from above.

He loved the dragons, and the skies were his home. Sunshine, fresh air, the world stretching out before him endlessly from the back of a creature that by all rights should never have to suffer itself with a rider. Maysie would have to understand that this was his life, and nothing would change it.

THIRTY

GRIFFIN STOOD WITH HER parents in the stronghold courtyard. The gate was open. Her older brother by two years, Skylar, and his wife, Zaina, were arriving home today after visiting her relatives and touring some of the other kingdoms. They had been gone for three months. Once they took over as the rulers of Drangrere, they wouldn't be able to travel for so long anymore.

There were a couple of roars, and Ruby, Emerald, and Jade flew over them toward the eyrie. Griffin shifted from foot to foot. She had so many things to tell her brother.

Griffin watched the gate anxiously. She clumped her turquoise dress up in her hands for a moment before forcing herself to relax and smooth it back down. Finally, they appeared. Skylar and Zaina walked hand in hand up to them.

Her mom and dad greeted them with hugs and kisses, and then Griffin finally got her turn. Skylar's beard had grown past his chin, and his blond, wavy hair was long enough to be in a half ponytail.

She grinned widely as she stared up into her brother's hazel eyes. "I missed you."

Skylar smiled. "Not as much as I missed my favorite sister."

They hugged.

"I'm your only sister, Sky, and don't you forget that."

Zaina had long, black, coily hair and green eyes. She was the daughter of farmers in Carodhall. Skylar had met her by chance during a festival near the border, and he had been smitten by her beauty and her kind heart. She was a year older than her husband.

"Sister," Griffin embraced her, "I'm happy that you're home. I hope you and Skylar had fun."

"We did. And we have plenty of stories to share."

"I have a few of my own, too."

They went inside, ate, and talked for a while. Zaina was tired and went to lie down. The king and queen had business to attend to, so Griffin and Skylar were left alone in the living room.

Griffin sat in an upholstered armchair. Her brother lounged on the sofa, enjoying a glass of wine. Sir Whiskers lay on the other end.

"Did Whiskers get fatter?" Skylar asked.

"He's not fat. He's a large cat."

"He looks wider than when I left."

Seeming to understand the conversation, Sir Whiskers narrowed his eyes at Skylar.

"Don't give me that look." Her brother reached out to pet him. The cat swatted at him and hissed. "Still as ornery as ever."

"Sky, there's something I want to tell you. I rode a dragon." She emphasized the last few words.

Skylar's eyebrows shot up, and his mouth fell open. "How did...you actually..."

Griffin nodded.

He leaned forward with curiosity in his eyes. "Tell me everything."

Griffin told him how it felt to ride a dragon and recounted her adventures from that day. She had waited until they were alone to keep some parts of the story a secret from their parents.

"The goblins are riding terror birds now?" Skylar asked.

"I saw it with my own eyes."

"Huh." Skylar took another long drink. "I would have never thought that they could be tamed."

"We once believed the same about dragons."

He nodded. "Remind me, was Erik supposed to be coming here for the going-away party?"

"No. It'll just be for our family and anyone who's invited. A letter arrived from him today, but I haven't had time to read it yet. Aunt Gertrude and Grandma and Grandpa can't make it. Grandma fell and broke her ankle. But they send their love." She stared at her hands for a moment. "I'm really going to miss everyone here after I move."

Her brother gave her a sympathetic look. "You'll have Erik and his family, and you'll make new friends. You're good at that."

"I'm not so good at leaving them behind." Griffin took a breath. There were more important matters to deal with. "Listen, we have to discuss the increasing threats to Drangrere. Attacks, especially by trolls, are on the rise because of how far and fast we're expanding the kingdom, and the new settlement defenses are ineffective. We need to go back to what we used to do. The dragon riders also need a new eyrie."

Skylar furrowed his eyebrows. "Why are you telling me this? What has Daddy said about it?"

"He won't listen to me. Before I leave, can you help me convince him to do all these things? I'm worried that something horrible will happen if we keep ignoring the threats."

"Griff, if he's not concerned, we don't need to be." Skylar yawned and sank deeper into the sofa. "He knows what's best for the kingdom. You don't want him to look weak and ineffective, do you?"

"No."

"Then don't worry about it."

She scoffed and rolled her eyes. Griffin didn't want to accept that she could do nothing. Zaina came in. She strode confidently past Sir Whiskers and cuddled up with Skylar.

"That's not fair," he complained. "How come you can walk by the beast without him attacking you?"

"Sir Whiskers and I developed an understanding months ago, dear," Zaina said. "I don't mess with him, and he doesn't mess with me."

"Did you enjoy your nap, my love?"

"I would have liked it better had you joined me."

It began with loving eyes and a kiss and then escalated into full-on making out. Seriously? With her sitting in the room with nothing to do but watch? Awkward. Griffin quickly left, rescuing her uncomfortable-looking cat along the way.

She went into her bedroom and set Sir Whiskers down. Then she picked up the letter from the nightstand and broke the seal. Her cat crawled into her lap, and she stroked him as she read.

My Dearest Love,

I'm excited that soon, we won't have to communicate by letters anymore. I can't wait to hold you in my arms again. In these past four months, my heart has been in agony at missing you.

I enjoyed your story about riding Emerald. Tell Kade that I thank him for keeping you safe. The dragons scare me. Don't tell anyone I said that. You'll have to show me how to be more comfortable around them.

I'm sorry that Alden and Onyx were killed. The riders here were also sad to hear about their deaths and mourned for them. I understand your frustration that your father won't take further action.

I wish I could do something, but if he won't listen to you or his captains, I doubt he will listen to a prince from another kingdom. Your concerns have inspired me to speak with the dragon riders here about what they see in their daily work. Their reports have been enlightening, and I look forward to comparing notes with you when you arrive.

But Drangrere is strong. The first one to put a dragon on its banners and to ride them. I believe your kingdom can withstand anything, and if aid is ever needed, Carodhall will stand with it. Both will soon be bound by blood, and nothing will break that alliance.

In happier news, our suite is prepared, and as you instructed, is ready to accommodate Sir Whiskers. I hope I can make friends with him, for my sake. He's so sweet with you. He can't be a truly mean cat.

Have fun at your going-away party, and give my love to your family.

Your True Love, forever and always,
Erik

Warmth spread through Griffin's whole body, and she kissed the letter. So many things had gone wrong lately, but Erik understood her and knew how to make her feel better. She lay back on the bed, held the letter against her chest, and lost herself in daydreams about what her life would be like in Carodhall.

Thirty-One

A S MUCH AS KADE didn't want to admit it, he was now, to an extent, becoming Alden. He sat at the table in the war room and studied the map that his late captain had created of all the recent attacks. Kade added the latest ones. Most were on the edges of the kingdom, although more were to the east and the south. Attempting to find a pattern was maddening.

Kade sighed and ran a hand over his face. He stared at Onyx's scale in the shadowbox. She and Alden couldn't die in vain.

Kenji walked in and gave him a concerned look. "Are you all right, Kade?"

"Yeah. I just can't figure out this map. If I stare at it any longer, it's going to drive me crazy."

The other rider sat next to him and slid the map in front of him. He stared at it for a moment, and then he shook his head. "I can see your point. I've heard talk that dwarves are reluctant to move to Hoeckan. They say that it's cursed. And some barons close to the wilderness are considering stepping down if the king continues to not listen to their concerns."

"Your drawing sessions always yield the best news and gossip."

"There are advantages to listening more than speaking."

"Cyril had mentioned that supplies Dally Springs needs to rebuild sections of the wall are slow to come," Kade said. "And one ballista that hadn't been destroyed was nonoperational. If someone suggests what can be done to help with the attacks or how to convince the king to take them more seriously, let me know."

Kenji nodded. "I'll keep my ears open. But the team is with you. We'll keep fighting."

"Finding a new rider for Crystal will help."

Shona walked in. "What are you guys up to?"

"Trying to find a pattern on this map," Kade said. He slid it across the table to her. "Here. You're good at stuff like this."

Shona leaned against the table and studied it. "How are things going with Maysie, by the way?"

"It's going well." Kade no longer felt the heat of embarrassment while speaking to his team about Maysie. He'd gotten over his first-girlfriend jitters.

"When are you going to bring her to the eyrie?"

"I don't know. I think she's scared of the dragons."

"She's still with you. That has to count for something." She traced the map with her finger.

"Hey, what happened to Roger?" Kade asked. "You haven't mentioned him in over a week."

"Riku's been asking if Roger liked the knife you had made for him," Kenji added.

Shona glanced at them and shrugged one shoulder. "We're not together anymore. He loved the knife that your brother made, but we decided we want different things in life. Time will tell if I'll find another man like him," she said glumly.

"You'll find someone, Shona," Kenji said. "Just don't give up."

"Thank you, Kenji." She gave him a grateful look. "Kade, I don't see a discernible pattern, but there are a few clusters. You could show those to the king. Instead of saying that he needs to fix things everywhere, start with a few spots. That should be reasonable."

"That's brilliant, Shona."

She smiled. "I wish Alden had let us help him."

"I know." Kade felt a dull pang of grief. He rolled the map up. "Now, I need to go to the captains' meeting. Can one of you take inventory of our storeroom? I think the food supply is getting low."

Kenji raised his hand. "I'll do it."

"And I'll find Jaheem or Barret and prepare for the afternoon patrol, sir," Shona said.

THIRTY-TWO

K ADE STRODE CONFIDENTLY INTO the council room, greeted the other captains, and sat when the king arrived. He gave his report and then held up the map.

"May I show you this, your grace?"

Magus beckoned him to come forward. Kade spread the map out in front of the king.

"This is a record of attacks throughout the past few months. You can see clusters in specific areas, especially on the southern and eastern borders of the kingdom. Respectfully, I would recommend sending more soldiers to help protect the settlements in those areas. Some of them take longer to fly to when they need help. Extra troops may deter trolls and goblins and prevent damage to the settlements and loss of life. Bogden said that we need to watch our borders."

Magus held a hand up. "I'm going to stop you right there. Bogden does not rule Drangrere. Although I am happy to listen to suggestions from my captains, the final decisions rest with me."

Kade bowed his head, and disappointment crept in. "Of course, my lord."

The other captains all wore expressions somewhere between amusement and frustration.

Magus looked at the map. "Some of these clusters are near key resources. Sending more soldiers to them would be strategic. After this meeting is concluded, coordinate with everyone else and see what can be done."

Kade nodded. "Thank you, your grace."

The other captains now had surprised looks on their faces. Kade walked to his seat, each step feeling lighter. Breanna patted him on the shoulder as he sat and gave him an excited smile. This was a step in the right direction.

"What of Hoeckan?" Magus asked.

"Work has started to rebuild it, again, and is going well," Vivek, the captain of the foot soldiers, said. He had black shoulder-length hair that had braids in it, a short beard with three braids under his chin, and brown eyes. The dwarf had plenty of battle scars that each had a story. "However, the workers and soldiers are nervous after the goblin attack. They won't stay in Hoeckan at night. They've requested more help to protect the settlement, and they are in the center of a cluster."

"All right. Send it to them. If it will get the coal mine up faster, give them what they need."

The rest of the captains took their turns to speak, and then Magus stood, as well as everyone else. "That'll be it for today. I still have plenty of work to do on my daughter's party. Everyone, remember that it's in two days, and you're all invited."

A soldier came in and intercepted the king. "My lord, a group of goblins has arrived with a load of leather and raw iron. But we weren't expecting another delivery until next week, and it was supposed to be minerals. They seemed to have trouble controlling their goats. The wagon was stuck under the overlook for some time."

The king shifted impatiently. "Are they from Bogden?"

"We think so."

"Then there was likely a mix-up. Let them unload their cargo. We can always use more leather and iron."

Before Kade could stand to roll the map back out, the other captains eagerly crowded around him. They congratulated him and discussed at length where to send extra soldiers. It was probably an hour or more before they finished. The brightness of the afternoon sunlight was fading into evening.

As the captains left, Vivek stared at Kade thoughtfully. "Alden chose his replacement well. I look forward to our continuing collaboration."

"Thank you."

Vivek gave him a nod and left. Kade stayed in the room for a moment. He hadn't wanted this or ever dreamed of becoming a captain. But now that he was coming to grips with it, the job wasn't so bad. And he could lean on his team when he needed them. There was no reason to handle every problem alone.

THIRTY-THREE

K ADE GRINNED WHEN RUBY purred and gently nuzzled Sapphire, who was sprawled out on the adult dragon's foot. The hatchling jumped to the floor and walked over to Emerald. The green dragon gave a friendly rumble.

"Good girl, Emerald."

Dragons generally weren't aggressive toward hatchlings, but it was a good idea to supervise the interactions. Sapphire looked at the open doors and scurried toward them.

"No, no, no." Kade ran over and scooped her up. The hatchling squirmed and protested loudly. "I know. I'll take you outside tomorrow. I'm not chasing you around when the sun's going down, and I have somewhere to be."

He walked her back to Ruby. "Say good night to Mama."

Sapphire nuzzled Ruby's nose. The red dragon looked toward the doors and made a noise. Smoky and Jade were returning from a late afternoon patrol. As much as he'd wanted to go, he had had to stay behind to meet with a few captains to study the map again. He put Sapphire up and came back out as Kenji and Barret dismounted.

"Anything noteworthy?" he asked.

"No," Barret said. "It was all quiet. I'm ready to have fun tonight."

Kade nodded. "Barring any calls, we should finally get a break."

Jaheem and Shona arrived with two carts of fresh hay. The team took care of the dragons for the night and then headed to their quarters to get ready.

Kade picked out nicer clothes for the party. A few months ago, Griffin had given him a black short-sleeved doublet, so he wore that over a dark blue long-sleeved shirt. The doublet had dragon embroidery in golden and blue thread. The pants he picked were so dark blue they were almost black, and he put on nice boots that weren't worn out.

Kade joined his team, and they all walked together. He and Jaheem dropped back a little from the others. The other rider had let his hair loose.

"Did you invite Maysie?" Jaheem asked.

"Uh-huh."

"Good. I'm happy for you."

Anxiety tingled through Kade. "I hope we don't get any calls tonight."

"Let's focus on enjoying the party, okay?" Jaheem wrapped an arm around Kade. "Don't worry about anything else."

Before he and Jaheem went into the great hall, they bumped into Princess Zaina.

"May I speak with you?" she asked Kade.

"Yes, my lady."

Jaheem bowed his head. "Excuse me." He went into the great hall.

Zaina walked a little way away from all the people. "Your name's Kade, right? I'm not good with names."

"Yes, Princess."

"Griffin has spoken about the attacks on the settlements and how not much is being done to combat them. I want you to know that when I am the queen, I will listen to any suggestions you have to keep Drangrere safe."

Kade raised his eyebrows.

She smiled. "Don't be so surprised. I grew up in a settlement. I understand the dangers firsthand. Even if my husband will be unconcerned about threats that don't directly affect him, I won't be." She looked around, and then she crossed her arms and frowned. "And he will have a threat that directly affects him if he doesn't drag his lazy feet over here soon."

"Thank you for your support, Princess." Kade bowed his head. "I'd better join the others." And not be in the middle of a couple's quarrel.

Kade entered the great hall. Bouquets of flowers of all colors, that were tied together with pink silk ribbons, sat in vases on trestle tables and adorned the columns. The tables were lined up on either side of the room. Musicians were playing, and the mood was lively and joyful. There were so many unfamiliar dwarves. Kade began to sweat. He searched the crowd for Maysie, but she wasn't here yet.

Griffin greeted guests at the other end of the room. He made his way there, sticking to the side near the wall where there were fewer people.

Her face lit up when she saw him. "I'm glad you made it." Griffin wore a red dress that had a silver flower pattern, as well as jewelry to match, and her dragon pendant. Just the tiara was silver with sapphires. She wore red dress shoes, and her hair was braided up into a bun.

"You look beautiful, Griffin."

"Thank you. I have something to ask you. When I make the trip to Carodhall, will you escort me?"

Kade grinned. "You're in luck. I was planning to. Barret can manage the eyrie while I'm gone."

Griffin let out a delighted squeal and hugged him. "Thank you. I know you'll keep me safe."

Kade noticed that Maysie had arrived. He bowed his head. "Excuse me."

This time, he had to work his way through the middle of the ocean of people to greet her. She wore a purple dress that Shona had once told the boys was called lilac, enough jewelry to make Emerald jealous, and purple dress shoes. Her hair was partly pinned back. She was also carrying a tiny box.

They shared a quick kiss, and he wrapped his arms around her. "I'm happy you came."

"I have a gift for you." She put the box in his hand. Inside was a silver pin in the shape of a dragon head with emeralds for eyes. "I assume Emerald is one of the green dragons I've seen flying around."

"She is." Kade smiled and pinned it over his heart.

Maysie had a soft, loving expression on her face. "It looks terrific."

Kade felt guilty. "I have nothing for you."

"That's okay. Spending time with you here is a gift. And I have someone to introduce you to."

She walked into the crowd and came back a moment later with two older dwarves. Kade recognized Odette. The man with her had long, wavy brown hair and a long beard that was loosely braided.

"You've already met my mom, and this is my dad, Quinn."

Kade shook hands with her father. "It's nice to meet you, sir."

Quinn looked him up and down. "Maysie's told us a lot about you. She also said that sometimes you seem unhappy in your job. If you ever get tired of the dragon riders, there's always a place for you in the mines."

Kade gave a friendly smile, even as he cringed inside. "Would you all like to sit down?"

They found spots at a table where they could sit across from each other. Wine was already set out, as well as snacks. Kade grabbed a glass.

Quinn folded his hands together and leaned forward. "So, Kade, I heard that you're not only a dragon rider but also a captain now."

"Yes. The promotion kind of fell into my lap, but I love it."

"I like a dwarf who works hard and can handle great responsibility. What would be your plans if you were to marry my daughter?"

Kade almost choked on his sip of wine.

"Dad," Maysie said in an exasperated tone.

"Well, it's an important question. He'd have to be prepared to balance family with dangerous and demanding work."

"Sir, right now, Maysie and I are taking our relationship one step at a time. We'll figure out each challenge together." But Quinn was right. Raising a family and being a dragon rider would be difficult. He hoped that if he married Maysie, they'd work everything out.

Odette put a hand on her husband's arm. "Dear, let's talk about other things tonight. My husband can be very outspoken, but it comes from a place of love."

"All right." Quinn grabbed a glass of wine.

Maysie grinned at Kade and held his hand under the table.

"Kade, do you like the dragon pin?" Odette asked. "Maysie spent many hours working on it."

"Yes, ma'am. I love it."

"Captain, I'm sorry to interrupt." A page stood behind him with a rolled-up message. "But you're needed urgently."

Oh, no. Not a call. Kade took the message, and his worst fears came true. A troll attack at Trinkelley Valley, the settlement farthest away on the eastern border of the kingdom. The party would be over by the time they returned.

"Do you have to leave?" Maysie asked with a frown, her eyes looking watery.

"I'm sorry. I'll make it up to you." He kissed her on the cheek. "You and your parents can enjoy the party. I'll come and see you tomorrow." Kade looked at her parents. "Sir, ma'am, I'm glad we spent time together."

"Be careful," Odette said with concern in her eyes. Quinn's arms were crossed, and his face was unreadable.

Kade grabbed a handful of snacks and went to gather his team. Shona was with her parents. She volunteered to fetch Kenji, who was sitting with his brother and some friends. Kade then went to find Jaheem and Barret. Both of them had a girl on each arm. He walked over and held the message up.

"No. We just got here," Jaheem complained.

"Can't we have one night off?" Barret said.

Kade shrugged.

"Well," Jaheem said as he looked at both of the girls with him, "it was fun while it lasted."

While they profusely apologized to their lady friends, Kade went to the head table where Griffin was sitting. Her cheerful expression fell when she saw the message in his hand.

"You have to leave, don't you?"

"Sorry. We have to go to Trinkelley Valley. Something about trolls."

Griffin gave him a soft smile. "Saving lives is more important than my little party. Fly safe."

Kade bowed, and she nodded back. Then he gathered his team, and they left the party and returned to the eyrie to go fight trolls and save a dwarf settlement.

THIRTY-FOUR

G RIFFIN STARED INTO HER wineglass, her sad face reflecting up at her. Kade and his team had a job, and they couldn't ignore it for anything. And if they all had to go, it meant the settlement was in a lot of danger. She'd tell the cooks to have a hot meal ready for the team when they returned. She pushed away her disappointment and went back to greeting guests. Her family joined her at the head table.

Once most of the dwarves had sat, her dad stood. "Ladies and gentlemen, thank you all for coming here tonight for my daughter's going-away party. Although her mother and I will be sad to see her leave in a couple of months, we could not have asked for a finer man than Prince Erik to be her husband, who will love and care for her for the rest of their days. Let tonight be about joy, celebration, and wishing a young lady good fortune and happiness, no matter where her life leads her."

Griffin kissed her dad's cheek as everyone clapped. "Thank you, Daddy."

His eyes glowed with love. "You're welcome."

Griffin stood. "I also want to thank everyone for coming. Drangrere will always be my home, and I will miss everyone here." She held her glass up. "So,

I propose a toast to beginning new journeys and never forgetting the old roads that take you to them. And to our brave dragon riders, who had to leave to defend a settlement."

After the toast, the main feast was carried in, and Griffin found her happiness again as she spent time with her family. Eventually, dancing started. Griffin downed the rest of her wine and joined the crowd.

She danced with friends and family members, bouncing back and forth inside between glee and sadness. Holding the party early was a great idea. She would have been even more of a mess if it had been the night before she left.

She was dancing with her dad and didn't notice the dwarf at first. Gasps rang out, and the crowd parted as a lightly armored soldier staggered through the middle of the great hall. He held his hands over a deep gash on his stomach, and blood dripped on the floor. The music ceased abruptly, replaced by frantic whispers.

Her dad approached the soldier. "What is this? What happened?"

The dwarf, a young man with blond hair and a short beard, raised his head. He opened his mouth, and a rivulet of blood ran out. "Goblins," he choked out. Then his face turned white, his eyes rolled back, and he collapsed to the floor.

Griffin gasped and held a hand over her mouth. Her dad looked too stunned for words.

"No. This can't be. This can't be happening. Not here," he mumbled and pressed a hand to his forehead.

Captain Vivek hurried over. "My lord, we need to act now and secure the stronghold."

There were shouts and the ringing of metal outside the great hall.

"Do whatever you have to," her dad said. Determination filled his eyes, and he pointed to a few guards. "You all take the queen and the princesses to their quarters and protect them. Hurry. And bring back weapons and armor for me and my son. Also, someone send word to the dragon riders."

The guards formed a protective wall around Griffin, her mom, and Zaina. They didn't have to go far from the great hall before coming across fighting. This wasn't a small incursion. Many goblin warriors and dwarf soldiers were locked in battle. How did they get in?

Griffin's heart pounded, and she wished she had a weapon in her hands. Several goblins came at the guards. They were from Raggerath. The goblins' armor had the grotesque motif of a dragon with curved horns. But there were other goblins with different symbols and colors on their armor and livery, too.

One dwarf guard was cut down, and the others pushed the girls on. Griffin tripped over the leg of a dead goblin and then slipped in a pool of blood. Tears stung her eyes. The screams of terror, the clanging of weapons, the reek of blood, and the horror of battle were suffocating. She wanted to curl into a ball, close her eyes, and cover her ears. But she couldn't.

Remembering the confidence Kade showed in the wilderness, Griffin focused on putting one foot in front of the other. She had to be brave. This wasn't the time to panic. Panicking would get her killed. As they neared their quarters, a group of soldiers ran in behind them to form a barrier, keeping the goblins at bay.

They made it, the door shutting securely behind them. A couple of the guards grabbed armfuls of armor and weapons for her father and brother and ran back out. The others split up to stand watch on either side of the door. Three iron bars were also lowered and locked on both sides.

Her mom collapsed on the sofa, breathing heavily. Her face was pale.

"It's okay, Mom. We're safe." Griffin wrapped her arms around her mom.

Zaina stood frozen in one spot, wringing her hands. Sir Whiskers ran into the room, his fur bushed up. He let out a scared meow. Griffin scooped him up and held him tight. The cat purred and rubbed his head against her chest, but his claws gripped her clothes.

Zaina left the room for a moment and then came back with a double-headed axe. She sat in a chair and shared a tense, worried look with Griffin. None of this should be happening.

Griffin walked into her bedroom and paced. They needed the dragon riders, but the team would be on the other side of the kingdom. A homing pigeon would take forever to fly out there, as long as the goblins didn't shoot it down.

She stared at her vanity, where she had little clay models lined up in front of the mirror. Griffin enjoyed playing with clay occasionally, even if, by the time the paint dried, her creations didn't come out exactly how she'd imagined them. Her favorite sat right in the middle. It was a purple dragon with a rider that looked like her. She ran her fingers over the dragon pendant.

"Griffin, this is the stupidest idea you've ever come up with."

She carried Sir Whiskers back into the living room, unhooked his claws, and plopped him next to her mom. "Please be nice to her for once. Mom, Zaina, I'm going to change, and then I want to be alone."

She may as well have not said anything. Her mom was too wrapped up in worry to notice that her daughter spoke or that Sir Whiskers was next to her. Zaina was equally distracted with looking toward the door. The sounds of battle could be heard somewhere outside.

Griffin hurried into her bedroom and closed the door. She took her dress and jewelry off and changed into warm clothes, boots, and armor. Her hair was in a bun, so she could skip to putting on the scarf and the helmet. She unrolled a map of the kingdom and located Trinkelley Valley.

Griffin slid her mirror out of the way. A sconce hung on the wall next to it. She pulled on the dragon head that was below the candleholder, and a secret door swung open. She grabbed her single-headed axe and lit a candle that sat on a chamberstick. Griffin hesitated at the door.

Her plan was dangerous, and she would be alone. But only she could do this. Griffin plunged into the dark corridor, shutting the door behind her.

THIRTY-FIVE

B ARRET WAS RIGHT. HIDDEN tunnels ran throughout the stronghold, some leading to exits outside that Griffin hoped the goblin warriors hadn't found. This was how she beat the boys to the eyrie. She used them often to travel around the stronghold in secret, taking shortcuts to different areas and rooms.

Besides the flickering flame of the candle, the only light was the eerie glow from pieces of minerals built into the walls. They were rare stones that shone in the darkness, but they only served as markers. Griffin ran as fast as she could without causing the candle to blow out. She held the head of her axe in front of it to break the wind.

The battle raged beyond the walls all around her, and she hoped no one would hear her. Then the clamor gradually grew less and less. Besides her family and the royal guards, few dwarves knew about the tunnels.

The dragon riders weren't part of that group. Griffin went up a few steps and reached the door that would open to the skywalk. A dragon head-shaped lever was next to it.

Griffin pulled it down and poked her head out the door. There were no goblins in sight, so she was safe to go to the eyrie. The outline of the door was hidden in a carving on the wall. She pulled the scarf down from her mouth, blew out the candle, and ran down the skywalk.

If any goblins had foolishly gone into the eyrie, Crystal would've turned them into ashes and dust. As she rushed in, she saw the white dragon crouched by the drop-off, looking out.

"Crystal," she called as she set the candle on the floor.

The dragon made a distressed whine and approached. Griffin rubbed Crystal's head, and then she ran to the big doors to look. She gasped. As many goblins that were in the stronghold, there was an army of a couple thousand or more outside. At least from what she could tell in the little moonlight that pierced the cloudy skies.

Fires burned in three settlements near the stronghold. The goblins shot flaming arrows into them. The attack was on a scale that they hadn't seen in Drangrere for a long time. Griffin leaned her axe against Crystal's saddle rack and then locked the eyrie and the nursery doors. The hatchlings squealed from the other side after they heard noise. They should be safe.

She ran to the white dragon's nest. "Crystal, come here."

The dragon, who was watching her curiously, approached. Griffin picked up the saddle, which was heavier than she thought. Crystal whined again.

"Come on, girl. We're the only ones who can do this. We have to find the rest of the team." Griffin looked into the dragon's pale blue eyes and hoped Crystal would understand how desperate the situation was.

The dragon gazed at her for a long moment, seeming to stare into her soul. Then Crystal went to her nest and crouched into the saddling position. She gave Griffin a look that seemed to say, "All right then. I'm ready."

Griffin had watched the riders enough times to know the process. Heave the saddle onto Crystal's back. Buckle the collar around her neck. Run two straps attached to a loop down her back, and buckle it behind her wings. Crystal lifted herself when necessary to help.

With that done, Griffin slipped her axe into a sheath on the saddle. Luckily, it fit. Then she grabbed the goggles and the harness that hung from the saddle rack and finished readying herself.

Griffin mounted Crystal and clipped herself in. She leaned forward and grabbed the bar on the pommel of the saddle. Memories of the last ride flooded her mind, and she hesitated. This was what she'd always wanted, so why was she scared?

The dragon turned her head and waited for a command.

Griffin took a deep breath. "Fly, Crystal."

The dragon stood and lumbered to the drop-off. Griffin braced herself for the leap into the night sky. Without Kade to hang onto, it was rougher, but she was more prepared. Crystal turned toward the fighting, but Griffin leaned right.

"No, girl. We have to find the others."

To her relief, Crystal obeyed. Based on the map, she just needed to travel straight. As they flew through the gap in the Cloud Spires, she hoped they'd return in time to save the stronghold.

THIRTY-SIX

K ADE DISMOUNTED. THE ATTACK hadn't been as bad as he thought. He'd expected six trolls, but two had been killed by ballista bolts, and two others ran when they saw the dragons. They had trampled a farmer's field, but the walls had held with minimal damage.

Dwarf farmers who were close to the borders of Drangrere stayed in the safety of a settlement at night. Ones in the innermost part of the kingdom lived next to their fields.

He was glad that everything had gone well. The team was fine, but they wouldn't make it home in time to return to the party. The other dragons landed a little way away to rest before their trip back to the eyrie. Kade started toward the settlement, but then something caught his eye on the tree line.

Thick pine woods surrounded them. Their boughs cast deep shadows onto the area below. The clouds made everything darker. Light from the settlement barely penetrated the edges, but there was a glint between two trunks for a moment. He grabbed his double-headed axe and walked closer to the tree line.

Emerald watched from a distance. An owl screeched. There was rustling but no more glints. Maybe the wind blowing limbs and vegetation around had confused him, or it could have been a firefly.

Nothing seemed to be out of the ordinary, so he turned around. Then something crashed through brush and tree limbs, and a roar sounded out. A large troll, wielding a dwarf spear, charged toward him. Kade's buddy had returned.

He jumped aside and fell to the ground as the troll thrust the weapon at him. Because the loop wasn't around his wrist, Kade lost his grip on his axe. Emerald rushed toward him but she wasn't close enough and he was on his back and defenseless. The rest of the team was even farther away. Everything went quiet as the troll loomed over him and growled. Its face lit up with triumph as it raised the spear.

Kade prepared to roll out of the way, even as he braced himself for the impact of the spear. Then a dragon roared above him, and he saw a flash of white. Kade scrambled out of the way as Crystal attacked the troll and killed it.

Stunned, he tried to gather his thoughts. Had Crystal followed them? But she had her saddle on and someone was on her back. The rider pulled the scarf down from their face. It was Griffin.

Anger bubbled up inside. Griffin couldn't take Crystal out for a ride whenever she wanted, just because she was the princess. But then confusion filled him. Why was she here and not at her party?

Kade ran up to Crystal. "Griffin, what are you doing here?"

"We have to go home now," she said frantically. "Nafrag's goblins are attacking the stronghold and settlements around it. They're already inside."

"Slow down. There are goblins inside the stronghold?"

"Yes."

Kade's heart raced. "Go tell the others while I speak with the baroness. When we get home, take Crystal to the eyrie and stay there." He pulled the spear from the holder on his back and handed it up to her. "Take this."

Kade quickly retrieved his old spear and the axe and told Baroness Freya that they needed to leave immediately. Then he mounted his dragon.

"Back home, Em. Fast."

Thirty-Seven

T HE FLIGHT BACK FELT as though it took forever, and Kade fidgeted in his saddle. How much devastation would they find at the stronghold?

Crystal kept pace with Emerald. Kade smiled at seeing the other dragon out in the field and acting more like her old self. She was ready for a new rider. As they approached the stronghold, the clouds cleared, but the air was thick with smoke.

Multiple fires blazed within Rownard, Dragon's Foot, and Lufken. Two farmers' houses had also been set aflame. The orange on the goblins' livery was everywhere, from the settlements to the land in front of the stronghold and flooding into it. There also looked to be other groups of warriors mixed in.

Emerald roared, and the other dragons joined in. Crystal turned toward the eyrie. Great. Griffin had listened. Kade focused on the battle.

He had never flown a dragon into war. This fight was on a larger scale than the ones he was used to. There had to be a strategy for dealing with the chaos below him.

His chest tightened, and his stomach roiled when he remembered that Maysie was trapped somewhere in this madness. The dwarves had to win the battle.

Kade pushed his panic down and scanned the ground. If he could break the goblins up into sections, the team could divide and conquer. Two large groups surrounded Dragon's Foot and Rownard, scaling the walls and attempting to break through the gates. They also shot fire arrows into the settlements. Lufken had already been breached.

Kade directed Kenji and Jaheem toward those groups. The rest of the goblins stretched out in a mass crowd in front of the stronghold. One group was attempting to break through the gate with a battering ram. They wore shields over their heads to protect them from arrows, but those wouldn't protect the goblins from dragon fire. He waved Shona toward the right side and pointed Barret toward the middle. He would take the left end.

Smoky scorched the goblins with the battering ram. The warriors shot arrows at him to hit Barret, but the gray dragon was too quick. Then the dwarf cavalry charged out. Archers provided cover fire from the top of the rampart, and soldiers formed shield barricades on each side to protect their comrades. Topaz strafed more goblins with dragon fire on the right side.

Dragons learned what the soldiers of their kingdom looked like, but there was a risk that dwarves could get caught in the crossfire. The legend about brave souls being reincarnated as dragons had better be true, for their sakes. Kade turned his attention toward his section of goblins.

"Fire!"

Emerald dived and left a river of flames through the middle of the goblin warriors. As his dragon turned to make another pass, Kade spotted them swarming up the side of the overlook, using rope ladders. So that's how they infiltrated the stronghold.

Then something whizzed past Kade's head. Emerald growled. The goblins had ballistae set up below the ladders to keep the riders back. There were three that he could see. Kade turned Emerald out of range as another bolt flew past them. How would they deal with those contraptions and not get killed?

The dragons couldn't attack them head-on. As Emerald burned another line through the goblins, Kade took another look at the ballistae. Something could be dropped on them if he approached from the side, using the overlook as cover. But that something would have to be large and heavy. And he would only have one chance to catch them by surprise.

Kade turned Emerald toward the mountains above the stronghold. She made a noise of protest and seemed confused about why they were leaving the battle.

"We're not retreating, girl. This will all make sense in a moment."

Kade searched for a cluster of boulders. He needed to get this done quickly. Then he spotted a few that were mostly round.

"Emerald, land right there." He directed her to the area, and then he pointed to a boulder that she could probably carry. "Pick up that rock."

Emerald grasped the boulder with her back feet and took a few extra flaps of her wings to heave herself into the sky. Streams of dragon fire lit up the night in the distance. Kade had Emerald fly toward the overlook. He'd have to time this right.

"Drop it," he commanded the second they passed over the first ballista. Kade looked over his shoulder and watched the boulder crash onto the ballista, sending pieces flying. Then it rolled over the others, smashing them into smithereens.

"Yes!" He pumped his fist.

Kade turned his dragon back toward the overlook.

"Fire, Emerald!"

She sent a stream of flames up and down the wall, fanning it with her wings and sending goblins fleeing or falling in fireballs. Then she burned what was left of the ballistae for good measure. The cavalry cut through the goblin ranks, and reinforcements on foot and on ponyback from other settlements arrived to help.

Their enemy turned tail and ran. Emerald enveloped retreating goblins in flames.

And that's how it continued. Dwarf soldiers pushed the goblin warriors out of the stronghold and the settlements and into the awaiting dragon fire. The valley glowed with each burst of flames. Part of the goblin army escaped but the stronghold was saved and the battle was won.

THIRTY-EIGHT

"**I** DON'T KNOW WHETHER to be angry or proud," Magus said.

In the morning, they had met up in the great hall, and Griffin had told her father how she'd snuck into the eyrie and ridden Crystal to find the dragon riders. They didn't know the count of the dead yet, but Nafrag's sneak attack had cost them many lives.

The time that a surprise shipment of cargo had come, it must have been goblins from Raggerath doing reconnaissance. The overlook was not well guarded and provided enough cover, along with the darkness from the thick clouds, for the attacking army to sneak in undetected.

The goblins had fired grappling hooks over the parapet. Kade wouldn't have been surprised if Nafrag had orchestrated that specific troll attack in Trinkelley Valley to lead the riders far away from the stronghold.

Walking past the bodies of soldiers and civilians was a difficult reminder of the cost of the king's complacency. Magus and Skylar only had minor wounds. Zaina and Helga had joined them in the great hall, too. Kade was tired, his clothes smelled like smoke, and he wanted to go find Maysie and her parents as soon as possible. He couldn't shake the icy dread at the thought that they might've died.

Griffin held her head up high. "Daddy, no one else could have ridden Crystal. I don't regret it, and I'd do it again in a heartbeat to save my home and my people. If I hadn't, we may not be standing here."

The king looked around the great hall somberly. Some of the wounded were being moved in to be tended to, where there was more room. "I'd say to not do it again, but that would be foolish of me because your actions saved us." He embraced her and kissed her head. "I'm proud of you."

Then he looked around at everyone with a resolute gaze. "To all my captains, we will meet tomorrow to discuss how to more effectively protect the stronghold and the settlements. Our enemies will learn not to underestimate us, whether it's trolls, goblins, or Nafrag himself." The king then headed out of the great hall.

Kade's team also left. He was about to go, but then Griffin approached him.

"Riding Crystal to come find us was brave," Kade said. "No one else could have gotten word to us as quickly as you did on dragonback."

"Thank you." Griffin then gave him her cute, pleading expression. "You know, there's still time before I leave, and Crystal doesn't have a rider yet. I could take her out again for some exercise."

"No," Kade said firmly. "We're already past the just one ride limit. I'm not pushing my luck."

Griffin pouted. "I suppose you're right." She looked over his shoulder and grinned. "Oh, you have someone who wants to see you."

"Kade?" It was Maysie.

He ran up to her and hugged her. "Are you okay? Are your parents safe?"

"I was so scared," she said in a shaky voice. "My parents and I locked ourselves in the back of the shop and barricaded the door. We heard horrible noises outside. A long time passed, and then one of my dad's mining partners came to tell us it was safe to come out. The goblins stole a bunch of the jewelry."

Kade looked away for a moment. "I'm sorry you had to go through that. I wish my team and I hadn't had to leave. I should've been here."

Maysie smiled. "But you all made it back and saved us. You more than made up for having to bail on me. Kade, I may not always understand what you do, but I promise I'll try. My dad will be harder to convince, but give him time."

"Thank you, Maysie. I love you, and I hope we can make this work."

"I love you, too."

They kissed, and Kade forgot how exhausted he was for a moment. He felt as if there was more hope on the horizon than there had been for quite a while.

EPILOGUE

G RIFFIN LOUNGED ON HER bed with Sir Whiskers on her lap. She ran a brush through his coat. Keeping his long fur mat free was a job in itself, especially after letting him run around outside.

She grinned as she remembered riding Crystal. Even though she'd been anxious while flying out to find the riders, being on the back of a dragon by herself had been exhilarating in a way she never could've imagined. She had already written a letter to Erik about it. But barring any more emergencies, that was her only chance to ride a dragon like that.

"Well, at least I still have you," Griffin said to her precious kitty. "And because you're not as dangerous as a dragon, despite what everyone else thinks, nothing can keep us apart." She held Sir Whiskers against her chest, and he purred and purred.

Two weeks after the battle, Kade and Barret patrolled the area around Hoeckan. They flew out there more often at the request of Captain Vivek.

It was believed that the goblins had entered the kingdom through the mountain pass in the Dragon's Tail. That was probably why they had previously attacked Hoeckan so that it would be abandoned at night when Nafrag's army moved through. They still had no idea if the goblin king had known about the party or if he had picked that night at random. And no one was sure if Nafrag had been present at the battle.

Magus was now in full support of sending any and all resources to every settlement for their protection and prioritizing stone structures. Soldiers would be posted at the overlook and any other weak points around the stronghold, and there were plans to build watchtowers in strategic locations so that no attackers could sneak in again. Drangrere's number one priority would be defense instead of expansion, which is what it should have been all along.

As they flew over Hoeckan, they saw that work was going well on the stone wall. The mountain pass was too large to build defenses around it, but protection around Hoeckan could be bolstered.

Kade turned Emerald to fly along the southern border, and Smoky followed. The best news of all was that Magus had given his blessing for a new eyrie to be built. A site just had to be chosen, and they wouldn't have to rehome any of the hatchlings. Alden's dreams would be realized. Kade was content in his role as a captain, and he had Maysie and his dragon. Everything was perfect.

They flew near the Dragon's Tail Mountains, and Kade checked the skies. If Syrene or Zallar or both showed up, he and Barret wouldn't be able to do anything without risking their lives and the lives of their dragons. They'd have to back off and watch.

He scanned the ground. A shape hid among some boulders on the slope of a mountain. It was a large, hairy-looking creature that stood on two legs, but it wasn't a troll. He swore he spotted horns. Kade turned Emerald to get a closer look, but by the time they passed by again, the creature was gone.

Smoky flew up alongside them, and Barret held his hands up in a gesture that said, "What?"

Kade looked one more time but couldn't find anything. He waved a hand to let Barret know there was nothing, but he would discuss this with the team later. Please let it not be a sign of more trouble.

Thank you for reading my book. Did you know that the majority of shoppers look at reviews of a product before they decide to buy it? So, I'd appreciate it if you left an honest review. Even one or two lines would suffice. See you in the next story!

About the Author

Lindsay McCafferty has always been a voracious reader and eventually fell in love with the fantasy genre. Years later, she became fascinated with dragons, especially stories about them not being enemies. She wrote *Axes and Wings* to be a fun and action-filled adventure for lovers of epic fantasy and dragons.

authorlindsaymccafferty.com

facebook.com/authorlindsaymccafferty

instagram.com/authorlindsaymccafferty

x.com/lindsaymauthor